Will had perched himself on the chair at the end of the table. He sat stiffly, tipping his head from one side to the other in the same way that Uncle Len makes Frozen Billy's head move when he's asking him a question. And Will had somehow made his mouth look big and square, and his eyes round and marble hard, like the dummy's . . .

Clarrie and Will live with their Uncle Len, a ventriloquist in the nearby music hall. But though Len loves his act almost as much as he loves his beer, Top Billing is out of his grasp until Will thinks up a way to double the drama . . .

www.kidsatrandomhouse.co.uk

ANNE FINE

Frozen Billy

Illustrated by Georgina McBain

CORGI YEARLING BOOKS

CORGI YEARLING BOOKS

FROZEN BILLY
A CORGI YEARLING BOOK 978 0 440 86630 5 (from January 2007)
0 440 86630 8

First published in Great Britain by Doubleday,
an imprint of Random House Children's Books

Doubleday edition published 2004
Corgi Yearling edition published 2006

1 3 5 7 9 10 8 6 4 2

Papers used by Random House Children's Books are natural,
recyclable products made from wood grown in sustainable forests.
The manufacturing processes conform to the environmental
regulations of the country of origin.

Corgi Yearling Books are published by
Random House Children's Books,
61–63 Uxbridge Road, London W5 5SA,
a division of The Random House Group Ltd,
in Australia by Random House Australia (Pty) Ltd,
20 Alfred Street, Milsons Point, Sydney, NSW 2061, Australia,
in New Zealand by Random House New Zealand Ltd,
18 Poland Road, Glenfield, Auckland 10, New Zealand,
and in South Africa by Random House (Pty) Ltd,
Isle of Houghton, Corner Boundary Road & Carse O'Gowrie,
Houghton 2198, South Africa

THE RANDOM HOUSE GROUP Limited Reg. No. 954009
www.kidsatrandomhouse.co.uk

A CIP catalogue record for this book is available from the British Library.

Printed and bound in Great Britain by
Cox & Wyman Ltd, Reading, Berkshire

For Cordelia and Russell

*I found the notebooks again
today, and read them through.*

The First Notebook

I *hated* Frozen Billy. I hated everything about him. I hated him even more than Will did, if that's possible. I hated his painted staring wooden eyes and the way his eyelids clicked when Uncle Len pulled the string inside his back, to make them blink. I hated his long thin legs, like dangling rods. I hated his bright red wooden mouth, clacked shut or gaping open as square and wide as the opening in a pillar box.

But most of all, I suppose, I hated his chirpy, over-confident voice.

You think that sounds mad, I expect. Hate a doll's voice? A wooden doll can't speak.

But Uncle Len is a ventriloquist. Oh, you never see his lips move, but that's because you're too busy staring at Billy sitting on his knee, blinking, and opening and shutting his mouth, and chatting, chatting – forever chatting.

I never minded him when I was little. I'm teased about the time I dared stamp my foot and scowl at Uncle Len. 'Make Wooden Billy speak!'

'Not Wooden Billy,' Uncle Len corrected me. He tapped the rusty tin label screwed along one side of the carrying box. 'See? It

3

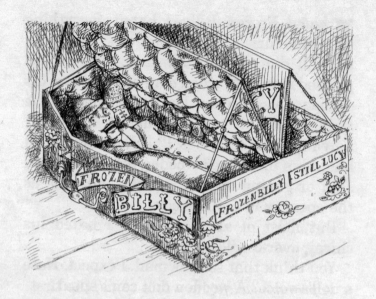

says here. His name is Frozen Billy.'

Will pointed to the label on the other side. 'And Still Lucy?'

'Yes.' Uncle Len ran a fingertip over the matching strip of tin on which STILL LUCY was painted in tiny white letters. He sighed. 'And if she'd been hanging on the same hook as Frozen Billy on the back of that Curiosity Shop door, I'd have a double act to send me straight to the Top of the Bill.'

He must have said it dozens of times over the years – usually when he was inspecting a fresh hole in his boot or counting his last few pennies. 'If I could only find Still Lucy, I'd be set fair for fortune.'

Mother would scold him. 'Come, now! You know as well as I do, Len, a man makes his own fortune.'

We all knew she was thinking of our father. He's in Australia, on his most important job yet, surveying a road through the outback, and saving every farthing (if they have farthings in Australia) to pay for our passages, longing for us to join him.

A brand new life! he wrote to us, the first week he was there. *You won't believe the wonders of this country. Mary, you'll be so happy. And Clarrie and Will will be in seventh heaven. Wallabies. Jacaranda trees. And heat, and sun, and huge wide skies, and everyone – everyone – building a brave new country.*

'All right for Charles,' Uncle Len muttered sourly. 'He always was the lucky one.' But after a moment, his natural good spirits returned. 'I'll just think myself lucky in his place while he's away, and eat his supper – if I'm invited, Mary.'

5

And Mother softened, of course, and let him stay. She can't help but be fond of Uncle Len, for all I used to hear her and my father whispering together about his faults. Uncle Len is a natural showman, with charm enough to fetch the ducks off water. That's why he works in music hall – luckily for him, because that meant he was usually still in his lodging house when Mother came home from serving in Mrs Trimble and Miss Foy's shop and, poking her head into the cupboard under the sink, called to me over her clattering of pots and pans.

'Clarrie, run along and ask Uncle Len if he would like to join us.'

I'd slam my schoolbook shut and run down to the alley. A few doors along, I'd push at his creaking boarding-house door and hurry up the stairs. 'Mother says there'll be plenty. Will you come?'

'Will I *come*?' He'd spin me round, even though, now I'm older, I'm no feather to lift. 'Will I choose to eat good food in fine company, rather than stone soup alone? Praise the day my dear brother married an angel!'

Uncle Len adores Mother. But, then again,

he really loves his brother, too. I've some-times thought he misses him almost as much as we do – like the night he reached for the cocoa tin and turned the picture of the girl on the front to face us.

'See her?' he said, nodding.

I didn't need to look. I spend hours gazing at her. She has the roundest face I've ever seen, all black and shiny, and she's all smile.

He tapped his finger against her perfect little teeth. 'Well,' he said, 'when Charles has earned his pile, and all our family is together again, we'll every one of us have a smile like hers.'

He heard me say something under my breath and looked up. 'What was that, Clarrie?'

I wasn't going to repeat the words I whisper to myself every night, and the hope to which I rise every morning: 'Let it be *soon*.'

I simply shook my head and I said nothing.

But we were happy enough – not as happy as the girl on the cocoa tin, but happy enough – until the day the telegram boy doffed his cap at my mother, and handed her a black-edged envelope.

Suddenly there was a flurry of tears and packing, and Mother was off to Ireland for Grandmother's funeral.

'Be good.' She hugged us tightly. 'Take care of one another. Uncle Len will look after you.'

We were expecting her back in a few days. ('Friday,' she'd said. 'Though, if the boat makes good time, you might even see me on Thursday.')

But, though we stayed up late, there was no clatter on the stair or rattle at the door. Friday passed, worried and silent. Saturday and Sunday, too.

'We'll send a telegram,' Uncle Len declared on Monday, though, since he had no idea who we should send it to, nothing at all came of that. But on Tuesday, as he was talking of going to the docks to get advice,

there was a knock on the door, a hurried
spell of whispering on the stair, and
suddenly Uncle Len was a man full of plans.

'We'll move Will back to his own bed, and
I'll put my stuff in your mother's room.'

'But surely Mother will be back any day –
tomorrow even.'

He let the silence drip. I thought I ought
to add, 'Won't she?' but Will was there first.

'Why? Why are you shifting things round?
What's happened?'

'Nothing,' he told us.

'So what was all that whispering?'

'Nothing.'

It took an age to worm it out of him. He
really didn't want to tell us. Something had
happened in Dublin. Either Mother was
wandering round in a daze after the funeral,
or there had been some awful mistake. But
she was suddenly 'under arrest', and then
'hauled up in front of the magistrate'. And
now, it seemed, she was in gaol.

'In *gaol*?' Will's eyes turned as huge and
staring, his face as pale, as Frozen Billy's.
'How can she be in *gaol*?'

Uncle Len shook his head. 'They say she
stole a basket full of food.'

'A basket of food? They must know Mother never stole a thing in her life – not even a length of silk ribbon from Mrs Trimble and Miss Foy!'

I bit my lip. 'They don't know anything at all about Mother,' I reminded him. 'There's no one there to speak for her. Now Grandmother's gone, there's nobody left in Ireland who knows her well enough.' I turned to Uncle Len. 'How long will she be away?'

He said he didn't know. 'Not long, I hope. A few weeks? Surely not long at all!' Will's eyes so spilled with tears he can't have seen the way Uncle Len's gaze swept round the room, avoiding mine. But even through my dry-eyed shock, I guessed my uncle suspected it might be a good while longer.

Later, when Will had cried himself into the deepest sleep, Uncle Len took me aside.

'You must write to your father tomorrow, Clarrie.'

Next day, I sent Will off to school, un-willing and alone. ('Mother would *want* it, Will.') Then I put on my best Sunday bonnet and went down to the corner shop. I pleaded with Mrs Trimble and Miss Foy until they agreed that I could take my mother's place at the counter to earn our rent until our father could get back to rescue us (though they said they would have to pay me less, because I was younger and had no experience).

Then I sat down at the table to write my letter. It was so hard to throw this black, black blanket over my father's shining dreams. It took all day. But when Will trudged home from school to see the envelope propped on the mantelpiece, he asked at once:

'A letter to Father? What have you told him?'

He saw the answer in my face and flew into a fury. 'You mustn't send it! I won't let you send it. No!'

'But, Will—'

'No!' Snatching it up, he ripped it in two. 'No! Father has to finish his job. If you tell him Mother's in gaol, he'll spend every penny he's earned on the first passage home. He'll end up spending it all. He might even have to borrow, and end up back with us worse off than he started – even deep in debt – just as Mother comes home again.'

How could I tell Will that, even coming from Australia, our father's ship might reach the docks long before Mother's? I just stood looking doubtful. But everything Will said to try to convince me was lifting his own spirits. 'Mother will understand! It's only a silly little basket of food she's supposed to have stolen. They can't keep her *for ever*. It can't be long, and Uncle Len won't mind. Each week he stays with us, he'll save on his own rent.'

Better this new, determined Will than the distraught brother of the night before. But I had another worry.

'How *can* Uncle Len keep this secret? Father is his *brother*.'

'How can he *tell* him?' Will countered fiercely. 'Uncle Len isn't going to *write*, is he?'

And it was true. Father has always said that one of the reasons Uncle Len slid into the music-hall world is because he found reading and writing so difficult. He would never ever manage a letter to Australia.

Sure enough, when he came home from the afternoon matinée, Uncle Len drew

12

me aside. 'Clarrie, have you sent the letter to your father?'

I couldn't lie, so I admitted, 'No.'

'Very well,' he said. 'But your handwriting's a whole lot better than mine. So set down this.'

Back I went to the table and sat obediently. 'Don't worry, Charles,' he made me write. 'As long as your little chickens are with me, they'll be kept warm, safe and fed.' And there was a whole lot more besides, because Uncle Len worships his brother. (I've heard Mother tease: 'If Charles told you to leap off a cliff, you would do it.')

I wrote everything he said down, as neatly and carefully as I could. We sealed the letter in an envelope and I addressed it, giving Will money for the stamp we both knew he wouldn't buy. Then Will took the letter straight past the post office down to the docks, where he tore it in pieces and dropped them in the harbour.

'I watched till the ink swam,' he whispered to me later.

So the only letter posted that week was the one Will sent to Mother, begging her not to let our father know that things were any different.

Please, please, he wrote, *don't worry about Clarissa and me. We will be strong and brave, and Uncle Len will look after us, I promise. And when it's all over, all of us can go together and start our brand new life, forgetting all of this.*

That last bit was so clever. I could as good as see Mother in the gaol, showing the letter to all the tough women round her, and them all taking Will's side.

'Got brains and sense, that boy.'

'What wouldn't I give for a chance of a new life?'

'Go on, Mary. Trust him. What have you got to lose?'

Somehow they managed to persuade her. So she kept writing her ever-loving letters to our father, making it all up about walks in the country, and people she'd chatted to in the shop. She slipped the letters inside ones she sent to us, and I kept back some of the money I earned to buy stamps to send them on to Australia along with the letters we wrote to Father.

And Father wrote back, full of excitement and love, with hundreds of plans. Will read the letters aloud, using his quick way with words to chop and change the bits that might lead Uncle Len to guess that the letter he made me write had never arrived there.

After, Will handed the thin sheets of paper to me, to send on to Mother. Sometimes I kept them one more night, to read the real words alone. Perhaps I shouldn't have done that, but I did. I think it was a sort of tax I charged for being brave, and hanging on, while we waited for the strange time of lying to be over.

*The Second
Notebook*

Everything went well at first (though the rooms seemed so cold and empty without Mother's cheerful humming, and the sweet smell of rose water that trails all about her). I made a brave fist of preparing the meals I'd watched her cook most often.

Uncle Len would tuck in. 'Excellent, Clarrie, my girl! Fine fare indeed!' He'd scrape the dish with his spoon, making a din like a stone rattling round a tin can, and when he caught me sternly eyeing him, he'd grin and wink. 'Come on, Clarrie. An empty sack can't be expected to stand upright.'

But sometimes, if the audience had applauded too thinly at the afternoon matinée, his mood was darker. I might frown at him for lolling his muddy boots on my polished fender, and he would make a face. 'Little Miss Disapproval,' he'd chide me. On days like these, he'd scowl at the burning coals till it was time to hurry back to the music hall for the evening show.

Will and I didn't fret. We knew all about Uncle Len's moods from whispers we had overheard. Father always said they happened when his act didn't go well. Uncle

Len feared he'd lose his place at the Alhambra Music Hall and end up where he'd begun, singing and telling old jokes in clubs while the working men pelted him with nut shells; or strumming his banjo at the end of the pier, rolling calf eyes at ladies he hoped might take pity and toss a few coins into his frayed cap.

And that would have been such a waste. Because, from the day he'd found Frozen Billy hanging on the back of that shop door and badgered Father into lending him the money to buy it, Uncle Len had worked so hard. He'd made good his promise to learn the art of 'throwing his voice' from scratch. He'd practised every day, and even risked the odd beating by sneaking into theatres without the price of a ticket, to watch other illusionists and pick up tips.

And soon he was a brilliant ventriloquist. He might lie abed for hours. ('Don't give me that fish-eyed look, Clarrie. You know I think the streets aren't properly aired till noon.') But the moment he lifted Frozen Billy from the box, his face took on a glow. He seemed to grow taller, and his eyes darted and shone. He was so skilled that he could keep the dangling wooden dummy blinking and shrugging and tipping his head to one side without anyone noticing his busy, busy fingers.

Even the theatre manager admitted it. One day, when we ran across her in the street, Madame Terrazini said, 'You have the makings of a great act there, Len.'

Uncle Len preened himself. And I knew why, because I've heard him saying it to Father often enough: 'Once Madame Terrazini takes you under her wing, you're set fair for fortune.'

'So I'll be moving up the bill, will I?' Uncle Len dared to ask.

Madame Terrazini didn't answer. She just kept smiling, and made to move on down the street.

'Soon?' Uncle Len persisted. 'A whole twenty minutes in the top half of the show?'

Madame Terrazini shook her head. 'I said "the makings" of a great act, Len. You have a thing or two to straighten yet.'

Again, she made to move on.

Stubbornly, Uncle Len grasped me tighter, to keep us all in her path. 'What things?'

Madame Terrazini met my eye. I knew she was uneasy about criticizing Uncle Len in front of Will and me. But, then again, I sensed she wasn't prepared to be bullied out of saying what she truly thought, just because he was holding us hostages to listen.

'Well,' she admitted finally, 'there is your terrible affection for the beer, Len. And though it's true I never see your lips move, night after night that dismal old patter lets your act fall flat.'

We knew about the fondness for the drink. We had heard Mother and Father speak sharply to him often enough. (He'd only laugh. 'Beer is the best broom for troubles,' he would say.)

But later, at home that night, Will dared to ask him, 'Uncle Len, what's "patter"?'

'The chat,' said Uncle Len. 'You know. What I say to the dummy, and what the dummy says back.'

Will was puzzled. 'What's wrong with your patter?'

Uncle Len scowled. 'Madame Terrazini thinks it's not witty enough. She says that it's dull and the audience gets restless.'

'Can't you go round the other music halls?' Will asked. 'Find the ventriloquist with the smartest patter, then copy it exactly.'

Uncle Len roared with laughter. 'Steal it, you mean? What, and have to look over my shoulder till the night that I find myself kicked in the gutter?'

Will shrugged. 'Invent a fresh patter of your own, then.'

'Easy for you to say! Talk pours out of you. Your mother says you could get a butcher talking about the price of herrings.'

I held my breath. Still, sometimes, talk of Mother had poor Will in tears. But that night he took it bravely. 'And I've a mouth as wide as Frozen Billy's, she says, that clacks open and shut just as often!'

I shuddered, glad it wasn't true for fear I would be haunted by my own brother. I watched as, sighing, Uncle Len laid Frozen Billy back in the long pine carrying box that looks like a coffin. (Oh, how I wished it were!) It was the dummy's face that haunted me. His cold dead staring eyes. They clicked shut the moment Frozen Billy was laid out flat. But sometimes, if I knocked the edge of his carrying box with my broom, they opened to stare. That's why, when Uncle Len went out, leaving the box lid open, I'd run to cover the dummy's face with the tablecloth from the cupboard. Mostly, when I heard Uncle Len's boots on the stair, I'd have time to whip it off again.

Sometimes I didn't.

'You've wrapped poor Billy in his shroud again, I see.'

'I was sweeping, Uncle Len. I thought it would keep the dust off.'

'You're a good girl, Clarrie.'

Everyone said that to me. The teachers, when I was at school. The vicar, when he gave me a prize (for 'Endeavour'). Mrs Trimble and Miss Foy. All, 'You're a good girl, Clarrie,' as if I were folded up, all clean and neat, like a handkerchief in a pile. No trailing edges. No bits sticking out.

But that's not how I felt. No. Somewhere deep inside, there was an explosion waiting to happen. I had the strangest dreams. I'd lie (all neat and tidy) in my bed. But in my mind's eye I was holding hands with Father.

We strode together over huge dry plains. Brilliant sunsets blinded us. Hot winds blew in my face.

'Look at it!' Father would be saying. 'A country as wide as a world. A place in which you can do anything. This is a land for fresh starts and brave people!'

My heart turned over and I could not wait.

I keep my dreams a secret. Will tells his. Like everything to do with Will and words, they are a conjuring trick, a razzle-dazzle. You're not sure if the picture rising in your brain is right, exactly; but you can see it, clear as paint.

He can write letters too. When I sat down to pen my lines to Mother, the words flew out of my head. How could I tell her how I spent the days after I left school to fill the place she left? I couldn't write of selling thimbles and cottons, then trailing home to black the grate and darn the stockings and scrub and clean and cook. How would it interest her to read of something that she knew so well? Who'd want to look at a picture of the back of their own hand?

So, though I never went to school again after the telegram came, and should have done my best to keep up with my learning, instead it was Will I set down every Sunday – and, if he was restless, some nights in between – to write to Mother.

Words rush to Will. He'd pick up the pen, stare at the wall for a moment, and then he'd be off, like a hare round the race track.

Today, Clarissa put on her best hat to go out, and Uncle Len chucked her under the chin. 'Clarrie,' he told her. 'You're such a beauty, you'd look at home under a silk parasol!'

Then Uncle Len stuck out his elbow. Clarrie rested her hand on his arm just like a lady, and they tripped down the stairs.

'It wasn't like that,' I reminded Will. 'What Uncle Len did say was, "Who do you think you are, prancing about in that fine hat? Lady Muck-on-Toast?"'

Will didn't even raise his head. 'Why should I worry Mother with Uncle Len's bad moods?'

His pen scratched on, leaving a trail of blots across the paper.

I couldn't help it. The words burst out of

me. 'His moods are almost every day now. And they're getting *worse*.'

Will kept on writing, but he answered me. 'That's because things are going badly again at the theatre.'

'But he makes Frozen Billy move and talk like a real boy. And no one sees his lips move.'

My brother shook his head. 'It's what Madame Terrazini said. It's the patter.'

I pointed to the letter Will was writing. 'That's all made up. You can write anything. Can't you help Uncle Len invent a new patter?'

He shrugged me off. 'How would I know what people want to hear? I've never even been in a music hall.'

'You could always make Mother and Father laugh. And me. And Uncle Len.'

'That's different. That's easy.'

'But you could *try*. And then perhaps I wouldn't have to be called Lady Muck-on-Toast simply for tying on my own hat!'

And I burst into tears.

Will shifted from his chair to the one at my side, and patted my arm. 'Now, now,' he soothed, the very same way Father used to do whenever I cried.

It made the tears fall faster. So you could say that everything that followed was my fault. If I'd not wept so hard, my loving brother would have simply kept on with his letter. I would have blacked the grate. And none of the rest of the story would be worth telling.

But I sat and cried.

The Third
Notebook

So that's how it came about that Uncle Len pushed open the door that night after another restless, cat-calling audience at the theatre, and caught me dashing tears from my eyes.

Tears of amusement.

For Will had perched himself on the chair at the end of the table. He sat stiffly, tipping his head from one side to the other in the same way that Uncle Len makes Frozen Billy's head move when he's asking him a question. And Will had somehow made his mouth look big and square, and his eyes round and marble hard, like the dummy's. And he'd been telling me, in the strange, cocky voice we think of as Frozen Billy's, what that rapscallion Will had been up to at school today.

Waving a stiff hand, he welcomed Uncle Len into the room. 'Step in. Step in and warm yourself beside the fire while Miss Clarissa here makes you a reviving mug of finest cocoa.'

Uncle Len fell in the spirit of things right away. 'Good evening, young Billy. And what's new with you?'

'New? *New?* What would *I* know about

new? Is this a new jacket?' Without un-stiffening his fingers, Will made a plucking move towards his other sleeve, just like the dummy would. 'Are these new trousers? Did you buy me a new cap? No. It seems the only new thing I'm going to get is a new patter. And that's *free*.'

Uncle Len hooted with amusement, then tapped me on the arm. 'Don't miss this, Clarrie!' He turned back to Will. 'So it's a complaint I'm hearing, is it?'

'It most certainly is,' Will said in Frozen Billy's voice. 'In fact, if you don't treat me better, I'm going to run away.'

'Run away, little man? Where to?'

Will cocked his head on one side, as though thinking. 'Let me see . . .'

And off they went again, with Uncle Len as glad as Will to keep the game going. He knew better than anyone how much time Will and I had spent over the years, watching him and listening to him practise. But still he seemed astonished that Will was able to ape Frozen Billy's voice with such swift skill.

'So you'll be a whole lot kinder to me in future?'

'I most certainly will, young Billy.'

'Cross your heart and hope to die?'

'Cross my heart and hope to die!'

'Stick a needle in your eye?'

'Stick a needle in my eye.'

'Jam a dagger in your thigh?'

'Eat a horse manure pie!'

Even Will's laughter sounded like Frozen Billy's. Maybe the mimic's art is one that lies in blood, and can be passed down, father to son, or uncle to nephew. Will had the voice so right. When I shut my eyes, it truly was like hearing the dummy speak through Uncle Len.

And clearly Uncle Len thought so too.

'Either you've taken pains to practise, or you're a born performer!' He turned to me. 'Is this how your brother has been spending the evenings, Clarrie? Pushing his school-books aside in order to take my place?'

'No, Uncle Len,' I assured him. 'Will does his lessons as he knows he should. This is the first time I've ever heard him speak in Frozen Billy's voice.'

'Is that the truth?' Uncle Len turned back to Will. 'That's hard to believe. To my ears, you're as good as an echo!'

And then, as if the very word had given him an idea, he went to the carrying box and flipped up the catches. As he pulled out the dummy, its spindly-trousered legs fell straight, giving Frozen Billy the look of jumping to attention. The eyelids clicked open.

Frozen Billy stared.

'Well, who is this?' Uncle Len made Frozen Billy say.

'Me? I'm your brother!' Will said in a matching voice.

Frozen Billy blinked. 'I knew I had a sister. Poor dear Still Lucy, missing these many years. But not a brother.'

'Not just a brother,' crowed Will. 'I am your long-lost twin!'

So you could argue it was Will, too, who fetched the sky down on our heads. There is no doubt it was his boast that sparked the idea that followed.

'Up on my knee!' said Uncle Len.

Will shifted off the chair onto the leg that Uncle Len stretched his way.

'Let your legs dangle. Looser. Looser.'

Will, being younger, isn't as tall as I am. And, though I'd never realized it before, once he is sitting on a knee, he's much the same height as the dummy.

Uncle Len winked. 'Now, Will. Think of something to ask Frozen Billy.'

Will pondered. 'How did things go at the Alhambra tonight?'

Frozen Billy cocked his head to one side. 'Not very well, I'm afraid.'

'How so?'

'I did my best. But still the audience sat woodenly in their seats.'

'Like skittles on a shelf, perhaps? Not bowled over by your wit?'

Frozen Billy blinked to cover the moment Uncle Len's lips were tempted by a smile.

My eyes were widening too. To watch, that first time, was the strangest thing. Soon, I thought nothing of seeing my brother engage in lively argument with a few cleverly carved rods of wood. On that first night, it seemed as if, because my brother was speaking back to it, the dummy truly had come to life.

I look back now and wonder why it took even the short while it did for Uncle Len to come to his decision: 'Will! This is too good to miss. You must join me.'

'Join you?'

'At the Alhambra!' He snapped his fingers. 'We'll do the act together. I'll get you fitted with clothes that suit.' His eyes gleamed more and more brightly and, tipping my brother off his knee, he rose from his chair and started striding up and down the little room. 'We'll work up a new patter, and show it to Madame Terrazini. She'll give me double the time on stage. The audience will love it!'

No point, I thought, in letting Will get caught up in Uncle Len's wild dreams. It was a merry enough idea to cheer an evening, but no way to live a life. I didn't dare come out with, 'And what do you think Mother will say when she comes home?' for fear that, tempted, Uncle Len might let drop how long that wait could be, and send my brother's good spirits tumbling again.

Instead I asked, 'And what about Will's schoolwork?'

Uncle Len made a face. 'What about it, Clarrie?'

I spread my hands. 'I mean, when is he to sleep? Over his books in school? The twenty-minute act is always the last of the evening, after all. We've heard you saying it often enough: "Top of the Bill – End of the Show!"'

Perhaps I did make the words sound a little too close to his own tones. In any event, he shot me a very irritated look. 'Perhaps there's one mimic too many in this family, Clarrie.'

I didn't let him scold me into quiet. 'Will's schoolwork must come first.'

Uncle Len snorted. 'Clarrie, his books can wait. Even old men can learn lessons, but how long will your brother look the same age and be the same height as Frozen Billy? Not for much longer. No, this is our chance, and we must snatch it!'

But I persisted. He'd talked of snatching things, so I snatched Mother's last letter off the table and read the lines at the end. *'And, Clarrie my dearest, I hope the time we're so unjustly kept apart will not be wasted. Keep to your books, my darling. And be sure to keep your brother to his. Then, when I step off the boat and hurry home, there will be time for all the hugs and kisses we are missing.'*

I swear I saw a sneer cross Uncle Len's face. 'Hugs and kisses! Clarrie, I'm talking *double money*. Don't you think we could all do with more in our purses?'

Will pricked up his ears. 'All?'

Uncle Len saw his advantage. 'Half the act earns half the money. Don't you believe that I'd deal with you fairly?'

Will sat bolt upright, staring.

'There's nothing *fair*,' I scolded Uncle Len, 'about dangling in front of someone who's never had a shilling of his own the promise of loud applause and easy money.'

And that was that. Two careless words had cost me the argument.

'"Easy money", eh, Clarrie? You think I come back here at midnight as fresh as a spring daisy?'

I could have said, as Mother might have done, that, since the Alhambra emptied at ten, it must be the nearby alehouse, and not work, that kept him out so late. But Will had already leaped off his chair and thrown his arms around him.

'I can do it, Uncle Len! I know I can. I can work every evening, and trade a beating at school each Thursday for slipping out to Wednesday matinées. And if Clarrie helps, I can keep up with my book work.' He shot a sly look my way. 'I won't end up leaving school as she has. And we can earn a whole lot more than she does, selling thimbles! Mother will be so pleased when she comes home. And Father so *proud.*'

That's when I lost the argument with myself. Will said the words 'And Father so proud', and suddenly a vision rose, startlingly clear. Will and I stood in a pool of coins and Father scooped us in his arms and said, 'All of this? Ours? Why, with all this we can make every dream come true at last!'

So that was that. I had become a co-conspirator, and Uncle Len and I were friends again.

The Fourth
Notebook

After that, it was all work. First, Uncle Len and Will spent hour after hour perfecting the patter.

Will came up with the ideas – mostly for knockabout misunderstandings and fights between two brothers. Then, like a man who has no skills as a cook himself, but knows which of the pies in front of him is likely to taste best, Uncle Len would pounce.

'Yes! That'll make them laugh to split their waistcoats. We'll work up that one, Will. That'll be a winner.'

They'd go over the lines together like two instruments trying to get more and more finely in tune.

'Which makes you laugh more? This . . . ?'

Uncle Len would direct Will with a finger. Keeping his jaw square and wide, my brother would spill out the words, then snap his bottom lip up like a trap.

'Or this?'

They ran through the joke again, slightly differently. 'Is it better that way?'

Finally, they turned to me. 'Hey, Clarrie. Which amuses you more?'

I broke off pulling pans out of the cupboard under the sink and watched.

'The way you did it first.'

'Well, what about this?'

When they were sure they'd chosen right, they went over it again, while I reached into the cupboard with the cloth. Under my fingers, suddenly, I felt a piece of board wobble. Dropping the cloth, I poked my head in further, just like Mother used to do. Behind the square of board under my hand was a place my fingertips fitted easily.

I pulled a little and the board came up. Underneath, beside the floor joist, lay a few coins, a pair of earrings I recognized, and Mother's wedding lines. I knew Mother wouldn't thank me for spilling the secret of her hiding place – especially to Uncle Len, who's so accomplished at 'borrowing' money when he feels in the mood for one more tankard of ale.

I let the board drop and shifted the pots and pans back on top.

'Give over with your endless clattering, Clarrie,' called Uncle Len. 'Come here and listen to us run through it all again.'

When they were sure the skit was at its best, they practised it over and over. Of course Will fell behind with his schoolwork. At first, I'd rouse him early and send him off – often with all his exercises done in my imitation of his hand, complete with ink blots, to save him from yet another thrashing. But after a few days I couldn't bear to pull him, still grey with the need for more sleep, out from beneath the covers. Promising myself (and the shade of Mother) that I would teach him better on Sunday to make up, I let him be.

And then, when Sunday came round, they'd be busy with the patter.

Until the day when Uncle Len declared: 'That's it, Will. Time to show Madame Terrazini what we can do.' He dropped a hand on my head. 'You'll have to come as well, Clarrie. You are a part of this as much as we are.'

I broke off laboriously penning my lies to our father – 'This morning, Mother said she might take us to the zoo on Sunday, if we are good. We hope to see some of the strange animals you write of so often' – and tried to wriggle out of going with them.

'Not me! What have I got to say to Madame Terrazini in an empty theatre?'

Uncle Len laughed. 'No empty theatres round here at seven o'clock, Clarrie!'

I stared. 'You're going to do it without speaking to her first? You're just going to step on stage and try the new show? In front of everyone?'

Was it my vehemence that made Will turn pale? Or did he have an inkling of bad times to come?

That first night, though.

Magic!

A few weeks later, everything about the Alhambra seemed almost commonplace. I knew all the acts backwards. In my sleep I could watch the contortionist twist himself into knots, and hear the ringing crescendo as the xylophonist whipped his balled sticks across the tin bars before tossing them in the air and catching them with a one-handed flourish.

I could tell which of the dancing belles had been snarling and snapping at one another in the dressing rooms even before they swarmed down the glittering staircase waving their feather fans, to start their high kicks and swirls. I knew the words of all the sing-along favourites, and how some of the magician's tricks worked (though I could never work out others).

But that first night!

Madame Terrazini found me where Uncle Len had left me to stand and watch, behind the stalls.

'Stage-struck, young lady? In love with my glorious Italian tenor? But here at the Alhambra, I'm afraid, the rule is, "No ticket, no show".' She bent closer. 'Wait a moment. Don't I know your face?'

I suppose I was frightened she might raise her voice and, even as the lights dimmed and the curtain rose, people might turn and stare. So mine wasn't the cleverest answer. 'I am Uncle Len's.'

'Uncle Le—? Oh, you mean *Len*!' She took me by the elbow. 'You've come to watch the show! And why not? Only a churl would ask a devoted niece to pay for a seat to see her own uncle.'

By now, she'd steered me through a tiny green felt-screened door I hadn't even noticed was behind us, along a narrow carpeted corridor and up a flight of stairs, soothing me all the way with her chatter. 'Especially when that same niece goes to the trouble of cooking Len's supper every night – and excellent it is too, if we're to take his word for it.'

I realized she knew my mother was away, and, guessing she knew the whole – and worst – of it, felt the tears rise and spill.

We stopped before another green baize-covered door. Resting her hand in the small of my back, she gave me a little push.

'Stay hidden behind the drapes,' was her last whispered warning before she left, 'or you'll have everyone craning to see why such a lovely girl sits all alone.'

I knew what she meant to tell me was, 'Here, you can stay out of sight. No one will see your tears, and no one will come to wonder how someone in such drab clothes can have a seat in the most expensive theatre box.'

So I sat well back, hidden by folds of velvet curtain, and in an instant all my tears were dried. It was like stepping into another world. The music! Colour! Lights! Laughter and warmth and magic. I was entranced by the dancers. *Nothing*, I thought, longing to drape myself over the curved shelf in front of me just to be closer, *nothing* could be more bewitching, more beautiful, more splendid than dance.

The girls swept off. On rushed a troupe of

acrobats who flirted with danger and defied the air. *No one*, I thought, *no one* could impress me more than these men of India rubber and steel.

On came a singer whose soaring melodies stirred the air around me. *Never*, I thought, have I felt my heart swell so close to bursting – and never shall again, till I see Mother and Father in one another's arms, with me and Will beside them.

And then, startling because the Alhambra had become another world, onto the stage stepped Uncle Len.

I heard the rustle of silk skirts as Madame Terrazini slipped in beside me.

'I've come to keep you company.' Lowering her bulk onto a chair, she leaned forward to nod to one or two of the audience I took to be nodding back at her, then settled to the show.

By the time the rush of blood through my ears had stilled enough for me to listen, Uncle Len had already introduced himself and Frozen Billy to the audience and settled the dummy on his knee.

'And what did you do today, my brave little young man?'

Frozen Billy's head tipped to one side, as if he were trying to remember. 'Today I went off to school—'

Uncle Len put on a startled look. 'I didn't know you went to school, Billy.'

The wooden hand shot up to touch the school cap. The tiny click it made could only have been heard by those with sharp ears in the expensive seats – and my poor brother, waiting nervously in the wings.

'Oh, yes!' The wooden mouth dropped open and clacked shut in time with the words. 'I've been to school for three whole weeks.'

The wooden head waggled. Uncle Len somehow tipped the school cap till it seemed to be slipping over one of Frozen Billy's eyes. ('Keep the audience watching the doll,' Uncle Len says. 'As long as they're watching the doll's face, they won't be watching yours.')

'Met any new little friends yet?'

'Yes.'

'Got a special friend?'

'Yes.'

'Boy or girl?'

Even to me, who knows his painted face better than I know my own, Frozen Billy appeared to bridle. 'Boy, of course!'

That's when I first noticed Madame Terrazini's sharp eyes move from the stage towards the audience, and realized I was hearing a ripple of amusement, no louder than a wave on sand, run through the theatre.

'Are you going to tell me about this little friend, Billy?'

'No, I'm not.'

'Going to tell the audience?'

'No.'

'Not even a clue?'

'No.'

And then, as if he were conducting an orchestra, from so soft I could scarcely hear to so loud I thought the roof might crack, Uncle Len whipped the audience into a frenzy.

'Do we all want to meet Billy's new friend?'

'Yes!'

'All of us?'

The roar was still rising. 'Yes! Yes!'

There was a bit more sparring to raise laughs, with Frozen Billy acting coy, then shy, then cross, then sulky.

'I don't believe you have a little friend at all!' cried Uncle Len. 'I think you made him up. I don't believe he's real.'

He turned to the audience and winked. 'Do you believe in Billy's little friend?'

'No!' they all bellowed.

'You don't think he's real?'

'No! He's not real!'

And that was Will's cue. That's when he had to step out from the wings and sidle on the stage. The audience howled with amusement to see him dressed exactly like Frozen Billy. His make-up even mirrored the paint on the dummy's face.

Will had to climb up onto Uncle Len's other knee. Then he and Billy had a friendly chat that turned into a blazing quarrel. Madame Terrazini barely glanced at the stage. The minutes passed, but she spent all the time studying the audience as the two painted schoolboys bantered on.

Frozen Billy got the best of the argument. Poor Will was made to look more and more of a fool, until the moment he slipped off Uncle Len's knee and stood, deeply dejected, with his head down and his hands in his short trouser pockets.

The audience roared with laughter.

Then, with each step he took towards the wings, Will somehow made himself look stiffer and stiffer. He let his lower arms dangle from his elbows, and lifted his upper legs high in order to take shaky steps that made his knees look as if they were hanging on strings.

He left the stage. The audience was applauding wildly, and shouting for more. Madame Terrazini was smiling.

Maybe I should have been delighted too. Maybe I'm mean in spirit: a bad niece. But I was furious with Uncle Len – furious that he could take my brother's generosity and cleverness and use it to turn the world so upside down that three hundred people could laugh and gasp, stamp and clap, and shout out, plain as anything, answers that would have you believe that the horrid grinning thing on his knee was quite real, and my real living brother was a stupid wooden dummy.

The Fifth
Notebook

nd you can guess what happened next. Uncle Len and Will were such a success that, inside a week, there was a flurry at the theatre. The glorious tenor stormed back to Italy in a grand huff, and Madame Terrazini gave Uncle Len the 'Top of the Bill'.

Next morning, Uncle Len tossed me a cloak he'd found in a pawnbroker's window. It was shabby, with a torn red silk lining. 'Here, Clarrie. Cut this to size so your brother can cover his braces and knicker-bockers on the way to the theatre.'

I darned it and hemmed it round (missing our mother terribly as I put on her thimble). Night after night Will snatched it up and swirled it round him with a theatrical villain's flourish. He'd ram Uncle Len's wide-brimmed hat down on his head to hide the cream and red pastes that turned his face into the mirror image of Frozen Billy's.

'Off I go, Clarrie! Off to help make our fortune!'

He said it with such cheer. Sometimes I leaned from the window to watch him prance down the street beside Uncle Len, turning each few steps to blow me yet another 'one last kiss'.

Later, much later, they'd startle me from sleep as the door creaked and in they came, hooting with merriment, reminding one another of the pleasures of the evening.

'Oh, Uncle Len! Wasn't it fine when that man in the balcony sneezed so loud I thought the chandelier might crack, and you made Frozen Billy say, "Bless you!"'

'But, Will, when you stumbled on your way off the stage, then made as if a string in your back had tugged you upright. That was masterly! Masterly!'

Sometimes I'd rise to make my brother a cup of cocoa to soothe him towards sleep. But sometimes, after long days of fetching and carrying heavy rolls of silks and trays of cottons, I'd stay curled beneath the coverlet pretending I hadn't woken, and hope their excitement would pass, and they would soon fall in their beds.

As often as not, Will was already yawning, half asleep. But Uncle Len would sigh, and stretch, then mutter something under his breath about seeing 'a man about a horse' before morning.

I'd hear the floorboards creak, and then

the door latch softly click. And I'd know he'd slipped out again, to go carousing.

The days went by. I wouldn't let Will say a word about the new act in his letter to Mother.

'She'll worry. And blame Uncle Len for keeping you from school.'

'No. She'll be glad I've worked as hard and earned as much as he has. *And* not spent most of it on gambling debts and ale!'

Mostly I kept my worries from my brother. But it popped out. 'He was never so bad when Mother was with us. Sometimes I think that only she and Father can keep Uncle Len in check.'

Will stirred the ink with his pen nib. 'Madame Terrazini said Len is so weak-willed, he'd spend the money for his own mother's funeral on beer and horses.'

'She said that to *you*?'

He shook his head. 'No. The dancers were talking while I was waiting in the wings. Mavis told Anastasia, and she just laughed and said, "The sooner their mother comes home and puts Len back in harness, the better."'

I sighed. Weeks had gone by. In every letter Mother said that each footfall ringing down the corridor, each rap on the cell door, set her hoping the prison governor had finally sent for her. Perhaps the lady who'd told the policeman, 'Yes, that's the woman!' had seen the real thief in the street and realized her mistake. Or woken in the night, murmuring, 'Now I remember! Her hair was fair, not brown. I was in error.' Any small hope, said Mother, to help her pace out each endless day in gaol, not even knowing if her quiet ways might earn her an early release.

I was trying to comfort myself as much as my brother. 'Perhaps it won't be too long now.'

Will gave me a long, unblinking gaze. Then, swivelling his eyes in their sockets, he clapped his mouth open and shut like Frozen Billy's. 'And won't Mother be astonished to see how her little boy has turned to wood!'

It never failed to make me shiver when my brother so imperceptibly made his body stiffen, and set his face as still as a porcelain doll's. He filled even Uncle Len with wonder.

'Will, you get better and better at playing

the dummy. The life drains from your face like water falling through a crack in a basin.'

Sometimes, though, Uncle Len seemed less at ease with Will's growing skill at ridding his face of all feeling.

'Don't stare at me in that cool fashion, please. It sets my nerves on edge.'

'Practice makes perfect, Uncle.'

'Your skills grow daily, Will. You have no need to hone them over supper.'

And it did seem to me there was a deal of truth in this remark. Each day, Will fell into the part with less of an effort. Even the time it took to ready himself for the show at the theatre grew shorter and shorter. And every night my brother needed less and less of that foul-smelling paste to turn his face dead pale.

There was a reason for this. Though it was weeks since he had risen early to go to school, bone tiredness did half the work. And I must have been tired too – too tired to see that weariness wasn't the only reason my brother no longer called out so cheerily, 'Off to make our fortune!' each time he left the house.

One night, I said it for him. The sharpest

look came over his face, though he said nothing. But that night, when the two of them came back from the theatre, I overheard my brother asking Uncle Len if he were sure there'd be a share coming his way. 'I work as hard as you,' said Will. 'And longer hours. You simply wear your own clothes and pat on a little powder to face the audience. I spend an age before each show painting myself to match Frozen Billy.'

Uncle Len tried to make light of it. 'So you'd be handsomely paid, would you, Will, for what any girl would do to her face for free? Be sure that, on the day I finally find Still Lucy, I will be offering your job to Clarrie!'

'Half the act earns half the money,' Will reminded him. 'Those were your own words.'

'I would be fair with you,' said Uncle Len, 'but half the money never seems to come.'

'What do you mean? Madame Terrazini pays you. I've seen her.'

'Oh, she pays me. The worry is, she pays me barely more than she did before. Certainly not enough to pay you.'

'But—'

I heard the chair legs scrape across the floor. 'Not now, Will. I have a man to meet in the Soldier at Arms, to talk about business.'

'Business!' scoffed Will. 'I see there's still money enough for beer in the Soldier at Arms, and a bet on the horses. Just not enough to pay your partner on the stage.'

Uncle Len laughed. 'We'll talk tomorrow, Will,' he said. And, with a clatter, he was down the stairs.

I left my bed to console my brother. 'We'll ask again tomorrow.' And the next night – and the next, and the next after that – I prompted, 'Go on, Will. Ask Uncle Len to speak to Madame Terrazini about his wages.'

Will simply shook his head – until the

night he lost his patience. 'If you're so sure that there's a point to it, *you* ask him, Clarrie.'

It took a day or two to gather courage. But the next Sunday morning, after bringing Uncle Len his porridge on a tray, along with a fizzing powder for his sore head, I spoke up.

'Uncle Len, it's been weeks.'

He lifted his head to stare at me with bleary eyes. 'Weeks, Clarrie?'

'Since Will left school to help you with the act.'

He went back to digging in the bowl with his spoon. 'He's a fine lad.'

'*Very* fine,' I said. 'But nights on the stage were not what Father and Mother had in mind for him.'

He scowled. 'Oh, indeed!' he said bitterly. 'Charles would want better for his only son than to fetch up in music hall like his own wastrel brother.'

'Uncle Len! Everyone knows you're a brilliant ventriloquist. The best!' I added the next words as gently as I could: 'But there was a purpose to Will's joining your act. And that was to help support the family.'

'I'm sure we all support the family, Clarrie.'

There was no other way to say it. 'I mean with his share of the earnings, Uncle Len.'

'Alas, Clarrie. As I've already explained,

even the extra wages barely stretch to cover my own needs.'

What lent me courage to persist was the memory of my poor brother trailing in night after night, so tired and dispirited.

'Uncle Len, while your "needs" include so much beer and so many bets on the hors—'

'Don't hector me!' said Uncle Len. 'Take your complaints to Madame Terrazini! Ask her how a man can move to the Top of the Bill and still be paid a pittance!' He clutched his head. 'Now out of the room, Clarrie! Leave me, before I lose my temper.'

Next night, Will sat with folded arms while Uncle Len gnawed at a fingernail with an anxious look.

'Not getting ready, Will?'

'Why should I bother to work?'

Uncle Len turned to me. 'Clarrie, tell your brother to get out of his pet and make haste to get ready.'

I spread my hands. 'He feels unfairly treated, Uncle Len.'

Outside, the clock tower chimes began. Uncle Len turned to Will in a panic. 'Hear that? The curtain will rise on an empty stage! What will we live on then?'

'On Clarrie's wages,' Will said stubbornly. 'As we do now, with most of your earnings going on your own pleasures.'

'I pay the rent!'

I might have spoken up then – 'Only part of it. And for so little of the food that we might starve.' But at that moment, hearing the last chime, Uncle Len dropped to his knees in front of Will.

'Do you really think I'd see you out of pocket? No! Every week I put aside a share for you.'

'So where is it?'

Uncle Len rose. 'Trust me!' he said. 'I am your only uncle. I love you dearly. I would do nothing to hurt you.' He stretched out a hand to take Will's chin in his fingers and turn the pale face towards him. 'Will, can you really look me in the eye and call me a liar and a cheat?'

Will tried. I know he tried. But Uncle Len had such a soulful, honest look about him that, after a moment, Will just broke away and stared in the fire.

And I? I let my brother down by standing by and saying nothing. And as I hurriedly helped him into his knickerbockers and shirt, and passed the jars of face paste, I let him down a second time. For in the moment Uncle Len turned away to pick up the carrying box, my brother was brave enough to whisper across to me, 'Do you believe him, Clarrie?'

And all I dared whisper back was, 'I don't know.'

Guilt turned to courage overnight. Next morning, I said to Will, 'I'm going to find the truth,' and went in search of Mavis and Anastasia. I found them cosy in a corner of the dressing room, busily lacing the bodices for the new cancan finale.

'Here's a long face,' teased Anastasia as soon as she noticed me. 'Have you strayed in the dressing room to tell us the theatre's on fire?'

'I have a question,' I admitted. 'About my uncle.'

They glanced at one another. 'Has he been unkind?'

'No, no,' I assured them. 'Though he can be a little irritable when he's tired.'

Again, their eyes met. 'Tired!' scoffed

Anastasia. 'More likely, when he's—'

Mavis frowned at her hastily, and she hushed.

I interlaced my fingers. 'Still, I was wondering . . .'

'Spit it out, Clarrie.'

'About his wages . . .'

Anastasia burst out laughing. 'Shall we guess Clarrie's question, Mavis? "How can my Uncle Len be Top of the Bill, and *still* come home each night with empty pockets?"'

They laughed again. I felt the blood rush to my face.

'So when he tells us Madame Terrazini pays him only a pittance more . . .?'

'He has a strange view of a pittance!'

'And if he tells us that he has put aside a share for my brother . . .?'

Mavis shook her head. 'Len's heart's in the right place, Clarrie. He'd truly mean to make good his boast. But then he'd hear some tip about a horse, and spend it all, and not even know how much he'd cost himself.' She leaned towards me over her lacing. 'Remember that, to your uncle, numbers are like alphabet letters. They fly straight out of his head. You could pour gold on Len, and he'd not thrive – not while he lives a few doors from the Soldier at Arms – without your mother's firm leash around his neck!'

I had my answer, so I crept away.

That night, I told Will, 'It seems Len's such a foe to numbers and such a friend to ale, he truly thinks he's poorly paid.'

And that was the end of the matter. None of us spoke of money after that. But from then on, it seemed as if the last of my brother's enthusiasm drained away. When Uncle Len said, 'Time to get ready, Will,' he'd scowl and delay, and from his mouth would come a tide of sullen muttering that Uncle Len was hard-pressed to pretend he hadn't heard. The very air in the house seemed to turn sour, and laughter vanished.

Once, as I was coming up the stair, I heard my brother's voice, fierce and tense. The door was open. I stood in the doorway, laden with groceries, and saw him leaning over the carrying box.

'Will, what are you saying?'

Hastily my brother shuffled back. 'Nothing. I was just setting Frozen Billy's collar in place.'

I could have told him, 'Will, I could hear from the doorway.' But what would I have said after that? 'I heard you say it, Will. Clear as a bell. "You are the very devil, Frozen Billy! If you were quick and breathing, I could free myself. But how can I ever kill the unliving?"'

The longer I thought about it, the more anxious I became. In my concern, I took to following Will and Uncle Len to the theatre each night. I'd clear the supper things, and sweep the rooms. Then I'd lock up behind, and hurry through the dark streets to get there just as the acrobats came to a finish.

Sometimes I ran into Madame Terrazini in the narrow carpeted corridor behind the stalls. She'd nod a greeting. I'd give a quick bob of curtsey in return, and hurry past to watch my poor brother grin and grimace his way through yet another show.

The act lasted twenty minutes – never less, and never a moment more. I think Uncle Len was ever mindful of Will's growing bitterness, and feared he might clamp shut his mouth the instant the last minute passed.

But the more Will glowered, the more Uncle Len's wits deserted him. Now, even when some wag shouted down from the cheap seats in the balcony, poor Uncle Len would stand and hesitate (while Frozen Billy blinked). It would be left to my sharp brother to think of something he could weave into the act to please Madame Terrazini with some fresh laugh, till the banter picked up again.

Still, Frozen Billy always won the argument. But by then I had usually left my hiding place – deep in the shadows at the back of the stalls if the theatre was full, hidden in folds of velvet curtain if one of the boxes was empty. I'd hurry down the carpeted passages and through the green baize door that is the barrier between those who pay to be entertained and those who are paid to entertain them, and come backstage.

So I was always there for Will when, clicking and clacking the wooden clapper hidden in his pocket to sound even more like a doll, he finally stumbled off the stage each night, the laughter ringing in his ears, and, falling in my arms, burst into tears.

The Sixth
Notebook

One Sunday I lifted the cocoa tin to wipe the oilcloth beneath, and found myself staring in envy at the girl with the beautiful black face and shining smile.

I turned to my brother, who was morosely churning out the weekly pack of lies to our father. 'Will, what would make you happiest in the whole wide world?'

He didn't hesitate. 'For Frozen Billy to fall under the wheels of a carriage and be broken in pieces.'

I clapped my hand over his mouth. 'Ssssh, Will!'

He tugged away. 'Oh, come on, Clarrie. Uncle Len won't be listening. He'll be dead to the world – *again*.'

I knew he was right because only a few minutes earlier I'd pushed the bedroom door open a crack. I was sliding in the boots that he'd left by the fender because I so hated it when he woke with a sore head, and started his fretful shouting. 'Clarrie, girl! Where are my stage boots?'

That always set Will scoffing. 'Stage boots!' And it was true that they were just a plain pair of hefty black lace-ups (though I could make them shine as if they'd been freshly lifted out of a shopfront display). They were nothing to compare with Will's perfectly round-toed shoes with intricate patterns of tiny holes, made especially to match the wooden ones carved on the feet of Frozen Billy.

I came to hate those shoes of Will's. I think it was because they were the last thing he put on before each show. While he was still daubing red on his mouth, or pulling on his shirt, I could still try to console him with talk of how soon Mother might be home, and how short the time would seem after that before Father had saved up the money for our passage.

But with the first click of those shoes on the floorboards, I found myself dealing with a wooden heart.

'Stuff your dreams in your pillow, Clarrie! For all we know, Father has found better things to do with his earnings than buy us tickets for the boat.'

'You read his letters, Will. How can you doubt him?'

'I think he sounds merry enough without us.'

'Why should he weep and wail in letters? After all, we hide our troubles from him.'

My brother turned on me eyes as hard as glass. 'How much trust do you have inside you to throw away, Clarrie? We wasted some on Madame Terrazini, thinking she'd pay enough for two. We wasted more on Uncle Len, thinking he'd share what he has. You carry on if you like, but my well of trust's run dry.'

I thought of arguing, though what would have been the point? Tears could have washed away stone faster than any words of mine could have cheered my brother. But next time I pushed the broom past the open carrying box, I found myself leaning over to hiss at the dummy in sudden fury, 'This is your fault, Frozen Billy! My brother changes day by day, and I blame *you*.'

The wooden lips lay in their wide, still smirk. The eyes were closed.

'I *hate* you, Frozen Billy!' I told the dummy. 'Each night you drip more poison into my brother's life.' I leaned even closer. 'But don't think you'll win,' I whispered. 'Remember this. You might spend night after night on stage with him. But what do

83

you know about me? Nothing! And if you don't know anything about your enemy, how can you hope to win the battle?'

To ram the message home, I banged the broom head hard against the table leg.

The eyes flew open. How Frozen Billy stared! I know he's made of wood, but I'll still swear I saw something in that stiff face I'd never seen before.

And it was triumph.

That's why I kept on following Will to the theatre. I felt as if I were locked in a duel for my brother's soul. For there were two Wills now: the loving, ever-hopeful boy my mother had left with me, and a cold puppet with a marble heart. If I weren't there each night to save my precious brother from Frozen Billy – wrap my arms tightly round him until his tears washed out the poisons of his act – I feared that somehow he might remain stuck for ever inside that queer little changeling doll he played.

One evening, Madame Terrazini dropped a hand on my shoulder as I hurried past.

'Clarrie.'

I hung my head, thinking she'd had enough of seeing me scuttle like a rat down her carpeted passages. 'Yes, Madame Terrazini?'

'We have some business together, you and I.'

I would have tried to find some way to excuse myself; but she could hear from the pattern of gasps behind that already the acrobats must be weaving their supple bodies into their last few astonishing patterns. In a moment they'd disentangle themselves for the last time and sweep off stage, leaving it free for Uncle Len to stroll on with his chair and Frozen Billy.

She saw my hesitation. 'Another time,

then. Run along and watch over your brother.'

Watch over, she said. Not watch, but watch over.

I stared at her as she walked off. How had she guessed?

But the answer came instantly. My brother had changed so much, no one could fail to notice. Even picking his way through street puddles two or three steps behind Uncle Len, he looked like an automaton. When people spoke, his eyes swivelled in their sockets and he held his questioner in an unblinking gaze. Sometimes it seemed as if he'd taught himself to slip through some small green baize door of his own between living child and cold, unfeeling figurine.

And just as a clock has no feelings about the passage of time ('So early!' 'Too late!') to distract from the purpose of telling it, so Will, it seemed to me, had turned himself into a grim and monstrous little doll, the better to play his part.

Even the act had changed. Day by day, so imperceptibly I scarcely noticed, a word changed here, a tone of voice hardened there, until I found myself shrinking behind the fluted pillar at the back of the stalls, sensing the chill that ran through the audience.

The patter somehow gathered a threatening edge. Now, when my brother spoke, it seemed that Uncle Len's eyes widened as much as Frozen Billy's. There was a sense of menace in the air, and laughs grew scarcer as the audience gasped at the cruelties spat out by two snarling puppets.

It made me shiver. But it was good for business. Seats filled on what were once the slackest days. The price of tickets rose, and still the people came in droves. There was talk round the town, till even over the long rolls of patterned Chinese silks in our little shop, the ladies were exchanging strange stories about the ventriloquist at the Alhambra and his sinister 'twin' schoolboys.

At home, there was a kind of truce. Will passed Uncle Len's plate along the table, or handed him the bread basket civilly enough. He answered questions about the neighbours who'd spoken to him on the stair, or how well he'd slept. But as he swung the cloak around his shoulders every night, he seemed to change. Sometimes he'd look at Uncle Len without a blink, and give a cold little smile as if to warn him, 'Be on your guard tonight.'

And sometimes, even from as far away as where I was standing at the back of the stalls, I could see panic in Uncle Len's eyes as he struggled to keep pert answers firing out of Frozen Billy's mouth. The shirts he handed me to wash came drenched in sweat now. The performance that had started in such hope and excitement was not really a ventriloquist's act any longer.

It had turned into something much darker and deeper.

One night, Uncle Len and Will slid into battle from the start. When Will walked out on stage, Uncle Len turned the dummy's head towards him as usual as he made Frozen Billy ask his first question: 'And what did you learn in school today, little brother?'

Will's answer was a fresh one.

'School? I've not been in school for weeks now.'

I could tell Uncle Len was startled. The

best response he could make Frozen Billy offer was, 'How so?'

And Will was ready.

'Because I have a wicked uncle who has somehow turned me into his slave.'

The audience chuckled, though you could tell they weren't quite sure what amused them.

The cold hostility in Uncle Len's eyes came out in Frozen Billy's voice: 'Slave?'

Will plucked at his schoolboy shirt and trousers. 'Don't be fooled by these clothes. What would you call it if someone was snatched out of school in his mother's absence, and forced to work and work and work, and be paid not a penny?'

Before some smart answer could come from Frozen Billy, and turn the joke, Will played Uncle Len's trick of bringing in the audience.

'Should you all think that cruel?'

'Yes,' called the audience.

'*Very* cruel?'

The audience called louder. 'Yes!'

'Very, *very* cruel?'

'Indeed!' they roared. 'Very cruel!'

'*Preposterously* cruel?'

How the audience laughed, to hear such a fine word coming from a schoolboy's mouth. 'Yes! Yes!' they shouted. 'Preposterously cruel!'

'*Monstrously* cruel?'

'Indeed!' they all shouted, and some wag called down from the balcony: 'Unconscionably cruel!'

Then they all started. 'Uncommonly cruel! 'Thunderingly cruel!' 'Shockingly cruel!' 'Devilishly cruel!' 'Unbearably cruel!' Even, from someone no more than a few rows in front of me: '*Damnably* cruel.'

'In short,' said Will, 'quite *unspeakably* cruel!'

The audience howled with laughter. Will turned to Frozen Billy. 'So, brother. What do you think this fine "uncle" deserves, for sitting both of us in splendour on his knees every night, but making one of us work with no pay?'

I saw the beads of sweat gather on Uncle Len's forehead. Will seized the moment to turn to the audience again.

'Should this kind "uncle" be despised for all his promises that turn to lies?'

'Indeed he should!' called back the audience.

'Perhaps he should even be thrashed like a scoundrel?'

'Yes!' bellowed the audience, enjoying the joke hugely.

'Arrested, even, for his false pretences?'

I saw the sweat run over Uncle Len's fixed smile as the audience roared their agreement.

'Yes! Yes!'

'Arrest him!'

Will tipped his head to one side in puppet fashion. 'No. Wait! I have a better idea . . .'

The audience waited, spellbound.

'I'll tell my mother! Yes! I'll tell my mother!'

They roared with laughter, and the act went on.

On my way backstage, I felt a hand on my arm and turned to see Madame Terrazini. She had a puzzled look. 'Clarrie, your brother surely cannot—'

I broke away. 'You must excuse me! I must be there for him when Uncle Len comes off the stage!'

I rushed off and waited, terrified, for the quarrel I was quite sure would follow. Smouldering with anger, Uncle Len strode to the carrying box waiting on its stand in the wings, hurled in Frozen Billy and left the theatre, ignoring both of us. I hurried after, dragging a grim-faced Will.

At the door of the Soldier at Arms, Uncle Len turned away without a word. Will muttered sourly, 'Ale drowns more men than Neptune,' and moved ahead of me. Each time I hurried to catch up, he walked even faster, till he was running. So in the end I let him go, and by the time I'd reached our rooms, he had pulled the coverlet over him to pretend he was sleeping.

Next morning Uncle Len greeted him with a scowl. 'Well, Will? Your humour last night sprang from some bitter root.'

Will stared back coolly. 'You know the saying, Uncle. "You should be careful what you give a child, for in the end you'll get it back."'

Uncle Len flushed. I thought the fur would fly. But there was something in Will's eyes that made Uncle Len hesitate. He looked quite frightened.

Pushing his plate aside, he sprang to his feet. 'I must be off. I have a man to see, and errands to run.'

In half a minute he was out of the door. Will calmly watched him go.

I lifted my brother's empty plate. 'Now it's my turn to ask: "Well, Will?"'

He only muttered sourly, 'I think, if Uncle Len wants a dog to follow him, then he should perhaps take the trouble to feed it.'

A few nights later, I woke to the sound of busy voices. Raising myself in bed, I listened through the darkness as hard as I could. The earnest talk kept on. I slid my feet out from under the covers and down onto the cold floor. I crept across the room, avoiding boards that creak, and poked my head round the door to hear, quite clearly, Frozen Billy's voice:

'. . . and I assure you it is the very hardest thing, to lose a sister.'

Then, from the same corner, came my brother's own tones.

'But, Frozen Billy, Uncle Len has looked for her in every curiosity shop and every pawnbroker's.'

The dummy's voice was angry. 'He must look *harder* and *longer*. Still Lucy must be *somewhere*.'

Then what a chill I felt! Here was my brother, lying alone in his bed, talking of a dummy's missing wooden sister in both his own and Frozen Billy's voice. I thought of shaking him from sleep. But then the horrid idea came to me that, startled, he might wake to find himself on the wrong side of that strange barrier between the dummy and the living boy.

I hurried back to bed and lay in the darkness, telling myself fiercely, 'Don't be so foolish, Clarrie! Frozen Billy's no more than a gangling toy, and children talk to toys.' I thought back to when I had a doll of my own, remembering how I had longed for her to

come to life far more than I'd feared it. I
thought of Mother, too, and tried to comfort
myself that she would have laid an arm
round my shoulders and whispered, 'Leave
Will to his dreams' (though in my heart I
knew it wasn't true, and she would have felt
the same horror as I did).

And then, a few days later, as I was tying
on my bonnet to go to the shop, Will called
from his bed to tell me drowsily, 'Oh, Clarrie,
Frozen Billy says you're to bring home some
thread the same blue as his jacket, so the
snag in his sleeve can be mended.'

I took him to be half asleep. But when I
came home that evening and tossed the

cotton spool on the table, Will said, 'Frozen Billy will be pleased.'

'Uncle Len, you mean,' I corrected him sharply.

'No,' Will said, idly enough. 'Frozen Billy.' Then, glancing up, he saw the look on my face. 'Oh, yes, of course!' he said slyly. 'It's truly Uncle Len I meant to say. I'm sorry, Clarrie.'

He stuck out his hands in a little 'I was mistaken' gesture. But his arms moved as stiffly as rods of wood, and, as I stared, he pulled his lips back to bare his pearly teeth like an unfeeling puppet.

But in his glass-hard eyes there was no smile at all.

You can imagine, my unease grew deeper till, one night, while Will was plastering the pale cream on his cheeks before the show, I heard a strange dull thud.

I looked up from the sock I was darning to see Will swivel his head to stare at the carrying box.

My eyes followed his. 'What was that?'

Will didn't answer, and I was still gazing at the box when I heard Frozen Billy's voice, all muffled: 'Let me out! Let me out!'

Will's hand, streaked with white paste, stayed, still as alabaster, in front of his face.

My nerves were jangling. 'Will,' I said sharply. 'Are you playing a trick on me?'

He turned his mask of a face in my direction. 'Trick, Clarrie?'

'Yes. Have you learned so much from Uncle Len that you can even fool me?'

He drew back his lips, but what I saw was not his real boy's smile. It was that set of fierce white doll's teeth. His mouth never moved. But once again I heard that same dull thud and muffled voice: 'Let me out!'

I felt such fright it almost came as a relief when Will gave a horrid sharp laugh. 'Why don't you do it, Clarrie? Open the box – if you dare. Perhaps Still Lucy has found her way home at last and climbed in on her side.'

I don't believe I would have found the courage, even to show my brother that the niece of an illusionist is not so easily duped. But just at that moment the front door banged, and we heard footsteps on the stair.

Uncle Len burst in, swaying. 'Ready to come, Will?'

I had another worry then. 'Uncle Len, have you been drinking?'

'I wet my whistle, Clarrie. That was all.'

'Before the act?'

He put on a sullen look. 'When I decide I want someone to nag and scold me, I'll look for a wife.'

He turned away as if the conversation was over, and picked up the carrying box.

'You've said it yourself a hundred times,' I persisted. 'Strong drink before the show is the fastest way to be shown out of the Alhambra theatre door.'

To get away from me sooner, Uncle Len tried to hurry Will by sliding a hand under his arm. But though Will jerked away and fell to one side like a puppet whose strings have gone slack, I'd still caught sight of what he was trying to hide.

'Delay the performance until you're on stage,' snapped Uncle Len. He threw the cloak round Will, and, grasping him by the shoulders, steered him out of the door.

I waited till their footsteps had died away before hurrying over to where Will had been sitting. Sure enough, there was the end of a strong cotton thread dangling loose from the dresser. It was a thread from my workbox, chosen so carefully it was almost invisible against the dark oak. I followed it along a crack in the wood to where it ended, out of sight on a low chair behind the side table, knotted to a muslin cloth wrapped round a stone.

I looked around the room. There on the sideboard was a wooden saltbox. I fetched it over and put it exactly where the carrying box had been standing. Then I tugged the thread.

There was a muffled thud.

I tugged again.

Thud!

I ran to the window and stared after my uncle and brother as they reached the end of our narrow street and turned the corner towards the Alhambra. My knees were trembling. I had the strongest feeling suddenly that everything in our lives was sliding further and further from safety and happiness. How disappointed in my powers of protection must my brother be that, trying to rid himself of the burden of being Frozen Billy's 'twin', he turned to such cold mischief? Pretend dreams! Invented commands from a wooden dummy! Now even a haunting!

I yearned for Mother and Father. They would have known what to do. I would have leaned out further and willed them on the stinging wind: 'Come home! Oh, come home, please!'

Except that Mother couldn't; and Father mustn't, for fear of wasting all the time we'd already spent apart.

Instead, I closed the window and turned back to the chilly, cheerless room. My only companion was the girl on the cocoa tin, smiling as calmly and seraphically as if she'd never known a moment of un-happiness in her whole life.

I loved her, but it still burst out of me.

'All right for *you*,' I heard myself whispering bitterly. 'You have no troubles at all. Things are all right for *you*.'

The Seventh Notebook

Our nights grew colder and darker, with sneaking winds that rattled the window frames and crept beneath doors. In his next letter, Father wrote:

Here, half a world away, we move towards summer. I think days can't get lighter, hotter, longer – and still they do! If only you were at my side, to hear the frogs in the creek, and laugh with the kookaburra. Oh, when will we be together?

'Never,' scoffed Will, tossing the letter down on the table.

I didn't argue. Will's world had turned as grey and unpleasant as the fog outside the window. Each night he found a dozen new ways of being sour.

'Herrings *again*? Clarrie, your mind's as cramped as this room. Can't you think of a new supper?'

'Clarrie, where are my shoes? Into which silly place have you tidied them this time?'

'This cocoa's thin as ditchwater, Clarrie.'

I told him shortly, 'It's the best I can do tonight.'

He scowled in the mug. 'Pass me the tin,' he ordered. 'I'll stir in more myself.'

Not even bothering to look my way, he stuck out his hand, fingers spread, and looked up in surprise as I dropped the tin on it. 'Empty? Can we no longer depend on you for *anything*?'

'We have run short of money again, Will.'

It seemed he was ready to quarrel about that, but in the end contented himself with swirling the drink with his spoon till it slopped on the rag rug. 'Ugh! Horrible! Horrible!'

'Which, Will? The hot drink I just made for you? Or the mess you've made for me?'

'Uncle Len's right,' snapped Will. 'You have become a nag and a scold.'

As if to prove ill-temper under a roof is catching, Uncle Len started on Will. 'Did I not ask you to find a rag to stop that hole in the window? There's a wind strong enough to lean on coming through tonight.'

Snarl, snap. Snap, snarl. I looked around and wondered how Mother had ever made a warm and welcoming home out of this dark, dank nest. Now she was gone, I saw it clearly. The bare boards were pitted and rough, the rag rugs fraying. The rented furniture had been broken and mended and broken again. Every mug was chipped, and all the chair covers worn and stained.

And Uncle Len was right. The spiteful draughts whistled through each hole and cranny.

How could we carry on in such a way? And yet I knew that the worse things were, the smaller the chance of keeping Uncle Len from spending even more of our money seeking solace in the Soldier at Arms.

When they had gone, I sat at the table and wept. Through falling tears, the smile on the face of the girl on the cocoa tin turned strange and quavery, like a face in water, as if, like the friend I'd made her, she chose to take my troubles on herself.

I tried to comfort her. 'You can't help me,' I whispered. 'You're just a painted face on an empty cocoa tin. You can't help me.'

But as I blinked away the tears to see her better, into my mind sprang the echo of something Uncle Len had once said, and the inklings of an idea that might save us.

*

Did Madame Terrazini even hear my nervous tapping? Or was it purely by chance that after a moment the door flew open.

'Ah, Clarrie!' she said as if she'd been expecting me. Ushering me inside her cluttered office, she shut the door behind us, pointing to one of the two flowery armchairs.

'Sit down.'

I perched on the very edge.

'So,' she said, smiling broadly. 'You've come for money at last!'

Now here was a surprise! Could she be offering an easier way out of our troubles?

I spread my hands. 'Well, if we could have just a little more . . .'

'*More?*' She raised an eyebrow. 'I assure you, Clarrie, the Alhambra has never paid their Top of the Bill as much as I pay your uncle and brother. Why, even my glorious tenor worked happily for less.' She sighed. 'No, I'm afraid if Len and Will want better pay, they'll have to look for another music hall to offer it.'

Why raise my hopes simply to crush them flat? If I'd not known the porridge jar was empty, the coal in the scuttle down to the last few damp lumps, I would have risen and walked out with my head held high.

Instead, I forced myself to say, 'I came to ask if you would very kindly let me borrow a few clothes from the theatre stores.'

'Clothes? For yourself, Clarrie?'

I nodded.

'Dresses?'

I shook my head. 'A bright blue jacket. A pair of knickerbockers. And, if I can find them, a pair of striped school socks.'

She raised an eyebrow. 'You seem a little old for dress-up games.'

'No, no. I thought, if I could find a jacket and knickerbockers to fit, then I could cut off my hair—'

'Cut off your hair?'

'As short as a boy's. Then I could take my turn on stage as Frozen Billy's twin.'

She stared at me. 'You? On stage, Clarrie? What would your uncle think of that?'

'I haven't told him yet. But he did once warn Will, "Be sure, on the day I finally find Still Lucy, I will be offering your job to Clarrie."'

Madame Terrazini chuckled. 'The day he finds Still Lucy! You are a family of dreamers, Clarrie!' Her face grew serious.

'I've heard that Mrs Trimble and Miss Foy work you hard enough. Why would you add to your burdens by taking your brother's place on stage?'

'To save him!' I burst out. 'He works night after night. His temper sours, and nothing cheers him. If I could take his place, then he could rest and his good spirits might return to him.'

She smiled at me. 'On stage to save your brother? Your lovely hair cut short? I tell you, you have the courage of a lion. A lion, Clarrie!'

My heart was lifting. 'So I may go in the storerooms?'

'Yes, of course.'

'And try to take Will's place?'

She spread her hands. 'Clarrie, your uncle knows his business. If you can satisfy him, I have no doubt you can satisfy me and the audience.' She sighed. 'Maybe it's for the best. Anyone can see that things are very wrong between your brother and uncle. Out there on stage the two of them seize every chance to snarl at one another and pick over ancient battles. You have the look of someone hovering over a sickbed, and scuttle away each time I remind you we have business to settle—'

That word again. 'Business?'

'Your brother's wages!' She waved a hand towards the huge safe standing in the corner. 'You can't believe I'd trust a boy his age to carry the amounts he's earned home in his knickerbocker pockets!'

'But surely, Uncle Len has—?'

'Uncle Len?' She threw up her hands in mock despair. 'Oh, Clarrie, would you have me watch your brother work so hard, only to see your uncle drink his wages away in the Soldier at Arms straight after? How could you even think it? Oh, my dear child!'

'But we *all* thought . . .'

Now she was staring at me as much as I at her. 'Small wonder, then, that your poor brother is in such a pet! I wonder Len hasn't put him straight, if only to improve his temper.'

'I don't believe my uncle knows. You see, you give him more than you did before—'

'A mere pittance more, I admit, now there are two of them to pay.'

'But more. Enough to confuse him into thinking that was the new wage for them both.'

She roared with laughter. 'Then Len's no better with his figures than with his letters, Clarrie!' Again, she chuckled. 'I'll leave it to you to turn your brother's growls to smiles. You've earned that pleasure.' Her face grew serious. 'Meantime, let's hear no more about you cutting off your hair and going on the stage.'

She drew a few notes from a drawer. 'Here. Take a little now to pay your rent and fill your larder. I'll keep the rest in my safe.' Pressing the money into my hand, she ushered me towards the door. 'If you are wise, you might prefer to keep this news from your uncle.' She put her arm round my shoulders and drew me near. 'But you can cheer your brother with the news that, by the end of this week, he will have earned—'

Lowering her head to mine, she whispered, then stepped back, laughing at the look on my face.

'That much?'

'Yes. That much, Clarrie!'

I tell you, I ran to the shop on air.

*

Mrs Trimble wiped the smile from my face.

'Late, Clarrie! Late! Don't think that you'll be paid for this first hour, since you've missed half of it. Now get to work at once. Customers are *waiting*.'

But even her scolding and her terse commands couldn't tether my mind to my duties. All morning I floated in a daze, sliding the heavy rolls of silk back in the wrong places, mislaying samples of elastic, scattering the thimbles.

By noon, Mrs Trimble had worked herself into such a lather of irritation, she wanted me out of her sight. 'Clarrie! You're of so little use today that you can carry these papers down to the Import Officer at the docks. Perhaps the fresh air will rouse you.'

It was a punishment. She knows I hate it when the sailors grin and whistle, and when the dockmen turn and stare. But she was right. The air was good for me. The cold winds filled my lungs and my head cleared.

Soon, I was standing on the quayside, watching a great steamship draw near. The old man clinging to the rail beside me shook out his pipe and nodded towards it. 'That's the *Stirling Castle*.'

'Castle?'

He saw my baffled look and chuckled. 'Her *name*. She's in from Calais.'

'Do you know all the boats?' I asked from politeness.

'No, no.' Again he chuckled. 'But I can read.' He twisted himself round just enough to wave at a notice board on the harbour wall. Behind a sheet of glass were pinned a dozen sheets of paper.

'In, out,' he told me. 'Sailings. Dockings.'

When he had shuffled off, I gathered my shawl around me in the icy wind, and went to stare. There, next to the ticket prices, was the list of ships due in and out of dock. Berthings from Singapore and Valparaiso. A sailing bound for Australia on Saturday, on the midnight tide. Another for Tierra del Fuego. If I am honest, I was looking for the name of the ship that I'd waved out of port two years before: the *Firm of Purpose*. I'd stood, tears burning, waving until my arm could have fallen from its socket, and my father was no more than a speck, and the ship little more than a dot, on the horizon.

The Customs Officer signalled me back inside his cosy warm office. 'Here, child. Give these to Mrs Trimble and warn her the next time her paperwork is so awry, she'll lose her rolls of silk for ever.'

What? Did he think, as Madame Terrazini does, that I've a lion's heart? I hurried back. Mrs Trimble snatched the import papers, broke open the seal and peered at the official stamp.

Satisfied, she turned back to me. 'So,

Clarrie, has the sea air cleared your brain of cobwebs?'

She kept me, to make up the hour I hadn't been in the shop. The clock was striking seven as I ran up the stairs and stumbled on the mat outside our door, sending it skittering sideways.

Out from beneath it poked the corner of an envelope. Dropped on the way to a neighbour's door? Or given to someone else by mistake, then passed back to us? I picked it up to inspect it.

It was from Mother.

I ask myself now how, knowing that Uncle Len and my brother were only a foot or two away, hungry for supper, I could have chosen so fast to clatter noisily up the next flight of stairs, to make them think I was only some neighbour passing the door on the way to their own room.

I think that – just for *once* – I longed to read the letter first, and by myself. I wanted to be first to hold it. I wanted to take my time to unfold it, and know that where my fingers rested, the last fingers to rest had been Mother's.

I read the letter and I cried and cried.

That night, I was so restless. Through my small window I watched the clouds scud over the sky and thought of the ships I'd seen straining at the tide, and of the voyage we all longed to make.

And finally, sleep came. Was it because Mother's letter lay hidden under my pillow that she was so vivid in my dreams? Singing under her breath; busying herself with her stitching as Will and I sat with our schoolbooks; gently scolding our uncle.

I woke to hear her voice ring round the room as clearly as if the dream were real. 'Oh, Len. You know as well as I, a man makes his own fortune.'

Then I heard my own voice in a whisper: 'Why not a woman, too?'

And as I lay, watching the silent moon dip and bow across the storm-bruised sky, I thought again of all the money waiting in Madame Terrazini's safe, of all the questions I'd asked her, and how she'd replied. And, for the first time since Will had climbed on Uncle Len's knee to play the dummy, I found myself wondering if – after all – some good might come of this talent for mimicry that runs through our family. In my mind's eye, in the dark, it suddenly came to me how my idea to rescue my brother from the music hall could grow and grow to be a veritable explosion of daring to rescue all of us from our waiting lives.

Would it work? Could it be done? And could I do it? Did I dare to try?

I'll tell you this: if you have been a 'Good girl, Clarrie!' all your life, you have one gift that no one else is offered.

You don't know where your limits are or where your boundaries end. Why, if you're brave enough, you might just find your wits as wide and uncharted as some brand-new country.

Like Australia!

The Eighth
Notebook

Mrs Trimble stared. 'Leaving us, Clarrie? Have you found better employment to keep the roof over all your heads?'

I kept my eyes on my shoes. 'No, Mrs Trimble.'

'Then is this wise?'

I offered her no more than a tiny shrug. She peered at me closely, then muttered something about 'ingratitude' and 'docking a day's pay, in lieu of notice'. I didn't mind. It made it easier to slip a length of shiny red ribbon – and one tiny thing more – into my apron pocket and feel no guilt. Threads we had in plenty at home. And since Mother was allowed to pick through the shop sweepings every night for scraps to mend our clothes, we had a basket overflowing with patches.

I didn't say a word at home, and no one asked. That evening, after Uncle Len and Will left for the theatre, I hastily put away the broom and followed at once. I was so close behind that, if they'd turned, I would have had to dart down an alley. They vanished through the stage door. I hurried in behind and, the moment I'd seen them turn towards the dressing rooms, went the other way, to the storerooms.

Each one is bigger than the three rooms we have at home pushed into one. They're all piled high. I slipped into the first, filled with the most extraordinary things: statues, guns, papier-mâché pigs, clocks, coronets, a stuffed dog, candlesticks, framed portraits. Think of each scene from every play or pantomime you've ever heard of – all the things on that stage, along with a thousand others, were in one or another of the storerooms.

I inched between a wheelbarrow and a large cardboard snowman. Behind a pile of swords, there was a box – WIGS, BEARDS, MOUSTACHES – under a pile of harem cushions topped with an Aladdin's lamp.

It took a while. Through cracked boards over my head thrummed all the tunes and drum rolls I knew so well. I searched through 'Props' and 'Wardrobe', taking my time, comparing, discarding. And as the acrobats finally bounced off stage, dislodging a host of dust puffs, I realized I'd found and borrowed – should I now call it stolen? – all that I had in mind the day the idea to rescue my brother came.

Next morning, I tied my bonnet as usual and hurried from the house. Nobody thought it strange that I carried a basket, and, if they had, I would have talked of bread or sausages I planned to buy.

Down at the docks, the sailors teased me, as I knew they would: first with whistles and smiles, and then, as I stitched all the morning in the bitter wind, coming closer to try to vex me.

'Who do we have here, shivering in her

thin shawl? Sweet Sister Suzie, sewing shirts for sailors?'

I peeped out from under my lashes, as I had seen the pretty ladies do when a boy they would like to be sweet on follows them into our shop.

A sailor the others called Jamie soon drew nearer. 'What are you sewing so busily, little lady? And why here in the stiff sea breeze? Have you no home to go to?'

I blew on my fingers to warm them for the thousandth time, and nodded at the customs office along the quay. 'I'm waiting for my papers – you know, the papers that must go with Mrs Trimble and Miss Foy's rolls of silk when the ship sails . . .'

'The bill of lading?'

'Yes, the bill of lading!' I said, as if I'd been trying to remember, not find out what I didn't know. I offered him a warm smile in secret thanks for giving me, with so little trouble, the first piece of information I needed. And I could almost see him scour his brain for something else to say.

'Odd, to send rolls of silk back over the sea when we've faced wind and weather to bring them here!'

'They're going on the *Fresh Hope*.'

'Then make sure Mr Henderson gets everything in order. Captain Percival is a stickler for paperwork.'

I'm not the first girl to claim I could have kissed a sailor – and probably with more cause than any other: two names without the asking. But I kept busy with my needle.

After a while, Jamie lifted the hem of my handiwork. 'The young lady who fits into this could do with a few weeks' growing!'

'It's not for a lady,' I told him. 'It's for a sort of puppet.' I sighed. 'But I have only a week to finish, and there's one part of it that, try as I might, I still can't manage.'

'Which part is that?'

I pulled a few bits and pieces out of my basket: a broken wooden spindle; copper wire; strong cord; two empty bobbins; and a bent metal shuttle.

The sailor stared. 'An odd collection of cast-offs. What did you hope to make from these?'

I had the answer ready. Maybe I can't make pictures easily with words, as Will can in his letters. But give me time and no one there to tease, and I can draw. The hardest

part was opening Frozen Billy's mouth to peer inside. After that fright – after my heart stopped thumping – I'd set to work and made my careful sketch of all the springs and coils and wires inside his head. Then, rolling him over in his padded coffin, I'd lifted the patch of clothing that hides my uncle's busy hand, and drawn what I saw in there, too.

'What's this?' asked Jamie, inspecting my first picture. 'A cave of fierce teeth! But what's all this inside?' After a moment's studying, he picked up the other sketch. 'Aha! So that's where the wire goes. What a clever little pulley. And these, I suppose, are tiny weights . . . But what's this spring for? And how does this bit work?'

Seeing him scratch his head, his shipmates drew closer, one by one. The argument started in earnest.

'Surely this spring must work with a balanced counterweight.'

'The merest touch here and look, the eyes would blink open.'

'With a deft finger, you could learn to lift this bar yet leave that one in place!'

And that was that. All week, I kept at my

stitching and embroidering, while in between their own tasks (and often, I fear, in spite of them) Jamie and Bert and someone from Santiago they called Luis chipped, whittled, chiselled, planed and buffed. They tossed my hopeless pieces of wood and metal over the quayside ('We've finer rubbish in our bilges, Clarrie!') and scoured ship's stores for other, better finds.

'Wouldn't these lengths of wood make good legs for your dolly? A bit of whittling, and she'll have ankles as fine as your own!'

'See? A prize coconut to hollow out for her head!'

'Gambling dice for her teeth. Last night I painted out every black dot on the ivory, and this morning they look perfect!'

'Look, Clarrie. The joints in your puppet's knees will move one way but not the other. One tiny drop of oil . . . *Now* can you see why I was polishing that ring of metal till it shone?'

At home, the snarling and snapping went on apace. I gnawed at a fingernail as, for the third time that week, Uncle Len snatched up the tub of lip paste and scolded, 'Will! I bought this only last week and already it's half gone! Can you be *eating* it?'

They were so taken with glaring at one another that neither saw my guilty face. I stole away, back to my bed, urging myself to be strong and keep my secrets one more week for all our sakes, whatever the cost to Will's spirits. Afterwards, I knew, the questions would rain down on me. 'How did you put it all together so cleverly, Clarrie?' 'Where did you find each perfect match?'

But, really, all I did each time I needed something was sit and think. And almost every time, the picture came to me of some small corner of the theatre storerooms, and I'd go running back. It was like hunting for treasure. I'd pick up the perfect bodice, and remember a pile of frilly aprons with the very same fine lace edging, tossed in a corner. I'd stumble on a heap of dancing shoes, and search till I came across ballet pumps the same colour at the bottom of a box marked THE BALLET COPPELIA.

All week I kept my secrets hidden. Each night I'd carry my basket home and try to cheer my brother by drawing out some small ham or sausage I'd bought with the money Madame Terrazini gave me. But I let neither

Uncle Len nor Will see that underneath, folded as flat as I could keep them, were my two sets of bright matching handiwork, growing and growing.

By Thursday, the sailors were done. And so was I. That night, as I cleaned Uncle Len's stage boots till they shone, I stole one last dollop of black dubbin to add to the cupful I'd kept hidden under the sink. And when my brother turned his back, I lifted one last smudge of red out of his tub of lip paste.

And I was ready. Hidden around me, under the mattresses, beneath the rugs, in the pillow case, and right at the back of the kitchen cupboard, was everything I needed.

Yes, I was ready.

I found Madame Terrazini in the Alhambra foyer, watching a man on a ladder polish the droplets of the chandeliers until they sparkled.

When I came close, she turned. 'Ah, Clarrie! I'm glad to see you.' She hurried me aside. 'Your brother still seems discontented. Have you let him sigh and scowl through yet another week, and still said nothing?'

'How could I tell him?' I burst out. 'Will's

smiles of triumph would have said it all. Uncle Len would have started with his charm and his promises, and by now all our gains would have been lost.'

She sighed. 'True enough.'

'But I have come to fetch the money now.'

'Why now, Clarrie?'

I said determinedly, 'I have a use for it.'

'But can you keep it safe?'

'It won't be with me long.'

Still looking doubtful, she signalled me to follow her into the office. 'Are you quite sure?'

'Quite sure.'

She gave a little shrug, as if to say, 'I tried my best.' Then, shutting the door behind us so no one could see, she made me face the wall until she had opened her safe. Sliding out trays of money, she laid them on the table and started to count.

In front of me, the piles of notes and coins began to grow. I couldn't believe the amounts of it.

She saw my face. 'What's earned is earned. Your brother worked as hard as Len.'

She finished counting and pushed the

heap towards me across the table. 'Clarrie, it makes me nervous even to think of you carrying all this away. Surely it would be safer to wait till your mother comes home.'

I tried my hardest to deceive her, but couldn't stop the first little twitchings of a smile.

She gave me another long and searching look. 'Clarrie? You have another secret, I can tell! You've had good news from Ireland!'

I kept my face set, but she wasn't fooled. Still, she didn't push me, either for truth or lies. 'You keep your secrets, Clarrie. You've earned them just the same way your brother's earned his wages. You've cared for him like a mother, and tried your very hardest to protect your uncle from his worst self. Really, I have to commend you. You've shown the courage of—'

Last time, she'd said 'the courage of a lion'.

This time, she paused, stared at the huge pile of money, stared at me, then finished up: 'The courage of a *pioneer.*'

Then what a weight rolled off my heart! She'd dealt with my family so fairly, I wanted to be honest and true in all my dealings with her. And now I knew that she had guessed at least a part of my secret. And from her look of wonder – of admiration, almost – I knew for certain she would be the last person in the world to try to stop me.

I scraped the wages Will had earned and she had saved for him into the pocket of my apron. 'You don't mind?'

'Mind?' She came round her desk to take me by the shoulders and kiss me warmly. 'Clarrie, my only wish is for things to go well for you and your family.' She chuckled. 'Oh! And, of course, that my glorious tenor will be free to return for the Monday performance!'

Back in the quiet of my room, I counted the money three times over. There was no mistake. Once I had thrown in Mother's few coins from under the sink, there was enough for what I needed.

One single passage to Australia.

All night, the rain lashed at the window-panes. I barely slept. My hopes were too great, and my heart too full. I watched clouds buffet the moon and listened to the scratching of rats behind the skirting.

And watched Still Lucy.

There she sat, propped safely out of sight behind the door. Under the silk frills of her bodice were hidden Mother's precious wedding lines. On her head was a wool wig covered with scarlet ribbons. Her patchwork skirt flared out around the tubes of fine brown silk I'd sewn to cover her legs. The prim little ballet shoes rounded off her feet to perfection.

But it was still her face I stared at most. Her huge embroidered eyes. The pretty tucks and gathers that made her pert nose. The painted dice of her teeth. The shiny black shoe dubbin of her beautiful wide cheeks. The bright red of her smile.

She had become the doll of my dreams as well as of Uncle Len's. For I believed that, when I had risen at dawn and sewn Mother's earrings safely under the pretty pigtails, this beautiful twin of the girl on the cocoa tin would help to make us all happy – give us smiles like hers.

*

Will took an age to wake. I handed him the envelope. Still blinking away sleep, he slid the letter out, unfolded it and started to read.

I didn't need to read it with him. I've known it off by heart for seven days.

My darlings! The best news! Yesterday I went before the Board. How they all glowered at me, and scowled at their papers, and picked at my answers till I trembled.

But all went well. I'm to be freed! How all my friends here cheered. All of them know how very much I've missed you. By Friday week, the prison gates will open, and I'll be running to the docks. The women send—

Will broke off reading. In the grey dawn light, his skin was silver pale, and his eyes huge.

'Clarrie? Is this—? Does this mean—?'

I laid a finger across my lips. 'Sssh! Uncle Len will hear.'

'He doesn't know?'

'Nobody knows – except for you and me.'

'Next Friday?' His whole face softened. His eyes filled with tears. For the first time in as long as I could remember, he looked like a child.

'Mother's to come home! Next *Friday*.' He whispered it again. 'Next *Friday*.' He touched my arm. 'Why, Clarrie, if there's a boat that night, she'll be with us the next day!'

He drew his knees up under the coverlet and clasped them as tightly as if he were hugging Mother. 'On Saturday!' he whispered. 'Only seven days!'

I put my finger back across my lips to warn him again to keep silent. 'No. Tonight.'

'Tonight?' He peered at me, then turned the letter over in his hand. 'Clarrie, how long have you had this?'

'Seven days.'

'Seven days! But every day without Mother has seemed like weeks. Why didn't you—?'

'Because,' I whispered, 'I had an idea. And what I needed was for you to be the self-same Will you've been all these past weeks.'

He hung his head. 'Have I been horrible? Oh, Clarrie! Yes, I have. I've been horrible, haven't I? Say it!'

'And you're to be horrible one more day, or

Uncle Len will see the difference and be on his guard, and my idea will come to nothing.'

'But with this letter in my hand, I don't feel horrible any longer.'

'Will,' I said sternly, 'are you Top of the Bill at the Alhambra, or aren't you?'

'Yes, I am.'

'And do the crowds come every night – and pay handsomely for their seats?'

'Yes, they do – not that we see a penny for it!'

I hid my smile. 'Never mind that now. You are a showman, just like Uncle Len. And today, you're to give the finest show ever.'

I climbed under the coverlet beside him, to explain the plan.

The Ninth
Notebook

I'm glad Madame Terrazini was in the theatre that night to wave me her fond farewell while everyone else was clapping. She raised her hand, and shook her elegant lace handkerchief as warmly and deliberately as if she were standing on a quayside, watching me sail away.

Would she have smiled so broadly if she had seen her brand-new 'Top of the Bill' twenty minutes before? I shivered and shook inside the side stage curtain I'd wrapped so carefully around myself. I didn't dare peek out as I heard Uncle Len come back to the carrying box he'd left ready beside where I hid. My limbs went cold with terror, and in my mind's eye I could plainly see the look on his face as he flicked up the catches and lifted the lid on Frozen Billy's side to find—

Nothing.

'Empty?' Was he talking to Will, or to himself? 'How can the box be empty? I put the dummy in myself, and we came straight from the house.'

I heard the cheers of the audience as the acrobats tumbled off stage, and, trusting in the confusion, parted the drapes just enough to take a quick look.

Uncle Len stood staring down at the carrying box. 'It was as heavy as usual! It rattled just the same! Where's Frozen Billy?'

He lifted up the box and shook it. Sure enough, from inside came a rattle and a thud.

'Of course!' Uncle Len's relief turned into irritation. 'Is this some prank of yours, Will, to switch the dummy to the other side and give me the fright of my life?'

He flicked the catch under the label that said STILL LUCY, and raised the flap on that side.

There lay Still Lucy, smiling serenely up at him.

'What the—?'

Behind him, the stage manager was coming closer. 'Len! The audience grows restless. Get out on stage.'

'But—'

'Get on stage! Now!'

Snatching up the dummy, the stage manager thrust her at Uncle Len and pushed him out in front of the audience. Uncle Len held Still Lucy at arm's length and stared at her in horror.

The audience laughed.

I've always said it: Uncle Len's a showman. It took him barely a moment to gather
his wits and say to the dummy, 'Well, here's
a big surprise!'

The audience laughed again.

'A girl, indeed! That's something new. A
girl!'

By now, with all eyes fixed on Uncle Len, I
had dared part the fold in the curtain just
enough to watch as he propped Still Lucy on
a chair, then prowled around her.

'A pretty patchwork frock! Nice smile!
Enchanting hair ribbons! And such delicate
red shoes!'

I knew what he was doing. He was taking the chance to walk round the new dummy and inspect her. He spotted the flap of loose material over her back quickly enough.

'Dear, are you comfortable?'

He reached out a hand, as if to settle her better on the chair. Slipping his fingers under the loose cloth, he found the hooks and pulleys the sailors had made to match Frozen Billy's exactly, and took a chance.

'So what's your name, dear?'

Still Lucy blinked her eyes.

'Shy, eh?'

Still Lucy nodded.

'Go on, dear. Be brave. Tell everyone.'

Still Lucy shook her head.

Was he unsure about the mechanism? Or was he worrying about the voice? To me in the wings, knowing how much sheer nerve Uncle Len needed (Suppose the mouth didn't open? Suppose it didn't shut?), it seemed an age of nods and winks and head-shakings before he took the chance.

'So, Little Lady. I'll ask you one last time. What's your name?'

My heart thumped. Jamie and Bert and Luis had pored over my drawings so carefully. They'd sanded and oiled so well. They'd tested every spring and wire a score of times, and taken advice from their shipmates. Still, I had never dared hope Still Lucy's mouth would drop open and clack shut as naturally as Frozen Billy's.

And yet it did. And the voice that appeared to come out of it was sweet and shy. Uncle Len even dared give her a lisp.

'Thtill Luthy.'

'Thtill Luthy?' Uncle Len teased.

The audience chuckled.

'No! Thtill Luthy!'

'Just what I said. Thtill Luthy.'

'No!' The mass of ribbons shimmered as Still Lucy's head shook. 'I thaid, "Thtill Luthy!"'

As Uncle Len's confidence grew, so did the audience's amusement. They couldn't take their eyes off the new, amazing dummy – so sweet, so pretty, with her shiny black cheeks and red, red lips and perfect ivory teeth. I glanced across at Madame Terrazini. Her lips were parted in wonder. It gave me confidence. I thought, if my uncle is such a fine showman that he can make even the theatre manager stare at the stage and not at the audience, then some of his talent *must* have come down to me. I know I can do it.

And I stepped out on stage.

I walked the way I'd learned from Will, picking up my black dubbined legs as though they were on strings. I let the shoes I'd stained bright red with stolen lip paste drop with a *tap, tap, tap* on the stage boards as I came closer.

As Uncle Len heard the laugh he'd been raising turn to a sudden gasp, he twisted round to see me coming.

But clearly nothing could surprise him now.

'Well, well,' he said. 'Still Lucy has brought her twin sister along with her. And what's your name, dear?'

Up until then, I hadn't thought of lisping. But I suppose I am a showman, too! Because suddenly I caught sight of the dancers staring at me in great amazement from the wings, and the funniest joke in the world occurred to me.

'My name ith Anathtathia.'

'Anathtathia?'

And off we went again. I was so up in the air with the thrill of it, I can't remember

precisely how the show went on. (Neither can Uncle Len, except for saying if I ever again bring him so close to nervous collapse, he'll have my guts for garters.) So all I can tell you is that we kept up the prattle like old hands, stumbling from one to another of the many old jokes he and Will had tried and discarded.

'So, Anastasia, you say you and Lucy live on a beautiful coral island. Tell us about life there. Does everyone work all week?'

In my excitement, I clean forgot my lisping. 'No, no. Since Robinson Crusoe was shipwrecked with us, all the work has been done by Friday.'

There was a moment's silence as the audience worked out the joke. Then how they roared!

'So how do you pass the time?' asked Uncle Len. 'Do you play cards?'

'No,' I said sadly, shaking my head. 'We have too many cheetahs on the island.'

More mirth. Then:

'Do you have grand feasts?'

'No. We have afternoon teas on the beach.'

'Why afternoon teas? And why on the beach, dear?'

'Because of all the sand which is there!'

There were as many groans as laughs, but Uncle Len kept on.

'And are there quicksands too?'

'Yes, but I won't tell you about them. It will take far too long to sink in!'

'You catch fish, surely?'

'Every day.'

'So tell us, Anastasia, which is the simplest way to catch a fish?'

I paused, looked winsome, and tipped my head to one side. 'Get someone to throw it to you!'

Uncle Len waited for the audience's laughter to quieten before bringing Still Lucy into the act again by making her ask me:

'Anathtathia, how ith our little pet goat?'

'Very annoying.'

'How tho, thithter?'

'Because it butts in such a lot!'

Again, we had to wait for the merriment to die down before we could carry on.

'And how ith our dear little pet parrot?' Still Lucy asked me next.

I made my eyes go even rounder, and my face turn sad. 'Alas, our parrot's very, very ill.' I made them wait before I finished up, 'I think it must need tweetment!'

As soon as the theatre was quiet enough to allow Still Lucy to be heard again, Uncle Len made her comfort me: 'Never mind, Anathtathia! Thoon our parrot will be well enough to fly higher than a houthe.'

'A house?' I said, stalling as I tried to remember the end of the joke. Then mercifully it came to me. 'That won't be hard. We've never seen a house that could fly at all!'

After that, Uncle Len asked me and Still Lucy what we liked the best about our new country.

'We're very cold,' I confided. 'So what we like best is that stuff – that stuff—' I cocked my head to one side, put a finger in my mouth and sucked as if I were a dolly, thinking hard.

'What stuff, dear?' Uncle Len prompted.

'You know,' I said. 'That stuff that changes colour three times in its life.'

'Three times?'

'Yes,' I said. 'It's black when you buy it, red when you use it, and grey when you've finished with it.'

'Coal!' roared the audience.

And on we went, with riddle after riddle twisted into jokes until we'd spent the time allotted, and a few minutes more. In the end it was Uncle Len who chose to roll some joke round neatly to match another, reached out a hand to draw me towards him as he held up Still Lucy, and made us both take a bow along with him.

The audience cheered and stamped and roared. The curtain dropped, swept up, came down again, swept up. We kept on bowing until I was dizzy.

The curtain came down one last time, and stayed down.

Uncle Len turned to me. 'Astonishing, Clarrie! A triumph! But how could you ever have—?'

Now came the *real* performance: fooling a man whose skill is fooling others.

I spread my hands. 'Don't blame me, Uncle Len. Will said it would be an excellent jape, and you'd enjoy it.'

Uncle Len held up Still Lucy to admire her. 'She is a splendid dummy.' He turned her round and lifted the flap to inspect her mechanism. 'Where did you find her? And was all this Will's idea? Was it his aim to make me die of heart failure?' He swung round. 'Will?'

The stage hands stood silent since, the moment the act began, every last one of them had seen Will snatch Frozen Billy up from where I'd hidden him when I switched the dummies, and lay him back in the box. They'd watched him pull a letter from his pocket, drop it on top, and run from the theatre.

Only the stage manager dared say it. 'Len, he's gone.'

'Gone?'

'Ran off the moment the act began.'

'A wise decision,' Uncle Len said wryly. 'He risks a thrashing when he gets home for tempting Clarrie into such mischief.' He turned the dummy back to face him. 'Ithn't that right, Thtill Luthy?'

No one laughed.

Uncle Len didn't notice. He went to the carrying box to lay Still Lucy safely inside.

There, on top of Frozen Billy, lay the short note I'd made my brother copy out that very morning.

Uncle Len stared at it blankly. To save his

pride, I picked it up and read it out aloud to everyone:

'"I'm sorry, Uncle Len. I've run away. I'm off to make my own fortune overseas. Your nephew, Will."'

'Run away?' Suddenly my uncle looked like a rag doll whose stuffing has dropped out of him. His jaw dropped as low as Frozen Billy's. 'Run away to *sea*? Young *Will*?'

I waited with heart stopped. Here was the test I'd dreaded. What would my uncle do?

For though Will could have played my part that night as puppet on the stage, I couldn't have played his as runaway. No one would ever have thought I'd gone to sea.

But this way, what a risk we ran. For Uncle Len might believe that Will had gone. But if he chose to remember only his sour moods over the last few weeks, he might say nothing more than, 'Damn the boy! He has been constant trouble! Now he must fend for himself!' and stride off to cool his temper at the Soldier at Arms.

Then he'd miss everything I hoped would follow, because this plan of mine depended on speed; and speed, here, hung upon a loving heart.

Give him his due, he didn't make me suffer long. I'd hardly caught my breath before he was seizing my arm.

'Will? Down at the docks? A boy so young? Clarrie, for God's sake, we must follow him!'

'Quick, then!' I said, my heart as light as air. For I knew, even if I failed in one thing, I'd managed another. I'd proved that, for all his petty sins and weaknesses, deep down my uncle's heart was true.

He stretched out a hand to hurry me, then

stopped as if he only now saw clearly that I was standing in a fluffy wig, peppered with ribbons, with shoe blacking over every inch of me and bright red lips.

'No time to waste,' he told me. 'I'll run ahead!'

Thrusting Still Lucy into my arms, he broke through the line of staring stage hands and ran like the very devil.

The Last Notebook

Here is a riddle that we missed on stage. How do you get four people onto one steamship with only one ticket? Uncle Len asked it a hundred times on the voyage, then answered his own question: 'Best ask Clarrie! For she is the only person in the world who has ever yet managed it!'

But it was simple enough, with everything set to fall into place like dominoes in a line. Down at the docks, Will kept his painted face well hidden in the hood of his theatre cloak as he waited for the boat from Dun Laoghaire. Through driving rain, he strained to pick Mother's face out from the throng of passengers leaning over the deck rail.

'Look for the clothes she was wearing when she went off,' I'd told him. 'Look for a woman in black.'

'But it was dark,' he complained to me bitterly after. 'And they seemed all in black. If I'd not had the sense to stand where I knew she'd pass, between the ship's berth and the quickest way home, I would have missed her.'

But it didn't happen. He had the luck to spot her as she hurried past.

He stepped up behind her. 'Mother!'

She stopped dead in her tracks. 'Will?'

She swung round, then clutched her hand to her heart.

'The fright he gave me!' she told me afterwards. 'To hear my own son's voice, then turn to see a living, breathing image of Frozen Billy grinning from the hood of a cloak. If I'd not been rooted to the spot in horror, I would have run a mile.'

But Will had not been able to stop himself. Forgetting his painted face, he hurled himself into Mother's arms. And as she felt his trembling frame through the wet folds of cloak, and heard him whisper, 'Oh, Mother!

How glad I am to see you!' she came to her senses and all fears fled.

They hugged and kissed, and then she held him at arm's length. 'Will? Why are you made up to look like a puppet?'

Behind them, a ship's hooter brayed, reminding Will.

'No time for that! Quick. You must get your ticket.' He dug in the cloak's lining pocket and pulled out the cocoa tin. 'Here is the money for your passage.'

Mother lifted the lid. Inside, stuffed tight, was all the money Madame Terrazini had given me.

'Will? Where does this money come from?'

'Father!' lied Will (though he claimed later that he was sorely tempted to ruin everything by boasting, 'My wages!'). And all the time he was pushing Mother back through the stinging spears of rain towards the shipping office. 'You must buy a ticket, Mother. The ship's about to sail and you must get on board.'

'On board?'

He said she stared at him as if he'd told her she must fly to the moon.

'Yes. We're off to Australia.'

'Tonight? But it's impossible. *Impossible!*'

She seemed so adamant, Will told us after, that he thought of launching into some sad tale about poor Father lying sick with fever, calling for his family. But then he claims he couldn't bring himself to tell such a cruel untruth, not even to hurry her on board. So he just stood there as the winds rose round them and the hooter brayed, insisting, 'We're going, Mother.'

She stood her ground, clutching her shawl to her in the furious wind. 'Show me *your* ticket, Will.'

He pulled out the sodden wet boarding card some happy traveller had tossed into the gutter at journey's end, and held it just outside the nearest circle of lamplight, so she couldn't read the printing. 'Here it is, Mother.'

Now Mother's face was poised between her soaring hopes and lingering fears. 'But what about my darling Clarrie? And Uncle Len! How can I step off one boat onto another without being certain every last one of my family is safely with me?'

What was my brother to say? For my plan's timing was so tight, with one boat in just as the next went out, that Uncle Len had yet to prove himself.

Will took a chance. As he himself said after, 'What's one lie more, when your whole roof is thatched with them?' He claims it was a stroke of genius. Mother says it was a dreadful risk to take, and Will should be ashamed of his foolhardiness.

I say my brother is the bravest, most daring and quick-witted boy who ever walked the earth. For Mother insists she heard him telling her, 'Uncle Len's on his way and Clarrie is on board.' Yet he insists, when Mother scolds, that she misheard, and what he really shrieked into the wind was, 'Uncle Len knows the way and Clarrie is on the boards.'

'Theatre boards!' he crows now, each time the story is told.

And Mother frowns and says, 'Luck shone on you that night.'

'Not luck,' he says. 'Clarrie's fine planning – and my astonishing performance!'

For, following my orders, he pushed Mother as far as the ticket office and, when she had her boarding card in hand, hurried her over to the sailors at the bottom of the gangplank. The first took her ticket, peered at it closely, then put out an arm to steady her as she grasped the swaying side ropes to start the climb aboard.

Will hung back a moment, as if to take the chance of one last lingering look at the city of our childhood.

Then suddenly he pointed at nothing and no one and cried excitedly, 'See, Mother? There is Uncle Len! See him?' Again he pointed, then turned back to Mother. 'Quick! You go ahead to find Clarrie. I'll wait here at the bottom of the gangplank and help Uncle Len with the bags.'

And Mother, longing to see me, left him there.

'What bags?' Uncle Len said ruefully, after. For when he reached the dock, he had not even a hat or cloak to shield himself from the blustering winds and sheets of dark sea spray crashing over the sea wall.

He ran from sailor to sailor – 'A young boy! Have

you seen a boy?' – while Will crouched in the shadow of a pile of crates, keeping watch for the sister he knew would soon be following, in a cloak far too large, and hampered by a box as long as a child's coffin.

I heard Will's piercing whistle even through the screams of the wind and the ship's hooter's steady warning bray.

'Clarrie! Over here, Clarrie!'

To save my frilly wig and painted face, I pushed back Uncle Len's cloak hood just enough to see where my brother was hiding before scurrying over the wet cobbles to join him.

I thrust the carrying box into his arms. 'Keep it safe,' I warned. 'And keep your face well covered.'

I turned to peer through the dark and rain at the milling dockhands urging the last few passengers aboard. 'Where's Uncle Len?'

Will pointed to a crowd of people hanging over the harbour rail, waiting to wave farewell to their loved ones. 'There, begging everyone to tell him if they saw a young boy slip on board any of the vessels in the harbour.'

I set off towards him. The wind lifted the

edges of the cloak with such force it fair blew me away.

I tapped my uncle on the shoulder. 'Uncle Len! Uncle Len!'

He spun round. 'Clarrie! For pity's sake! Have you seen him?'

Nodding, I pointed up the gangplank of the *Fresh Hope*. 'Oh, Uncle Len,' I wailed. 'He's gone aboard!'

'What? Did you watch him go?'

'The sailors turned their backs, and he ran on.'

'Did he, indeed?' Uncle Len peered hopefully between the swaying shafts of light that fell from the *Fresh Hope*'s portholes. 'We're out of luck, Clarrie. They're at their posts again.'

Another warning blare came from the hooter on the first of the ship's mighty funnels.

He stared at me with haunted eyes. 'Clarrie, your mother left Will in my charge, and if he goes, her heart will break! No good to tell her that I came too late! Too late to find the captain!'

'What shall we do?'

'Do? Only one thing to do, Clarrie!'

And without the least hesitation, my brave uncle charged at the gangplank.

As he hurtled past, one of the sailors reached out. But all he took in hand was Uncle Len's billowing sleeve, and the cheap theatre silk tore so easily that all he was left with was a handful of wet cloth.

At the top of the gangplank, Uncle Len darted a look first one way along the deck, then the other, then vanished through a pair of rain-lashed doors. And though the two sailors at the bottom of the gangplank seemed to make great play of waving their arms and opening their mouths wide, I fear their enthusiastic cries of 'Stowaway! Stowaway!' must have been totally blown away by the wind, for the sailor at the top appeared quite deaf to their warnings.

Now, one by one, the last of the ship's crew finished their tasks on the quayside and hurried aboard. The dockhands loosed the cables. And as the powerful little tugs turned to their task, the great boat began pulling at the last of its moorings.

I ran back. 'Will! They're laying hands on the gangplank. Time to go!'

And from my bodice I slid out the last, and strangest, of all my treasures:

A perfect bill of lading, carefully signed by

the Import and Export Officer, Mr Henderson, and stolen by me the day Mrs Trimble punished me for leaving by setting me to file it along with a hundred others. You don't work all day with fine fabrics without learning how to remove the stains that spoil: soot, blood – and even ink. So in my very last hour in the shop I'd dabbed away with my tiny little pad of bleach to wipe out both the name of the ship and its commander. And, a little while later, in my own good time, I had refilled the blank space so neatly: Name of the carrier: The *Fresh Hope*. Under the command of: Captain Percival – and made one or two tiny alterations more – until this official form was turned into the very passport of happiness.

And now I held it stiffly between my fingers. And Will and I were ready to do our training at the Alhambra proud and make the grandest show of things. I only wish that Madame Terrazini could have been there to watch as we faced one another and let our cloaks slide to the ground.

Now, with our painted faces and colourful dolls' attire, we looked a strange pair indeed.

Will picked up the carrying box as if it

were our travelling suitcase. Stiffly, he offered me an arm. Stiffly, I took it.

Together we made our eyes go huge and round and expressionless, and stepped out like puppets from behind the crates. In the wind, only the two of us could hear the eerie tapping of our feet on the cobbles as we picked our knees up high and made our way over to the sailors unlashing the gangplank.

We came up close. Will swivelled his eyes in their sockets to hold one sailor in a steady gaze as the other one ran for our cloaks. Twisting my upper body, I bent from the waist to drop the bill of lading from my stiffened fingers into his hand as we went past.

He smiled. But my face stayed as still as painted tin, and so did Will's. We never blinked. Arm in arm, we took our tiny mechanical steps ridge by ridge up the gangplank.

A call came down. 'What says the bill of lading?'

But it had been easy enough, with a pen twist, to change, not just the date on the paperwork, but also the words 'two silk rolls' into 'two silk dolls'.

And if there was a wink from the sailor at the top as he cried, 'Gangplank away!' then I'm the last to tell. All I will say is that those three grand seafarers, Jamie and Bert and Luis, kept to their story.

'Two quite amazing dolls, Captain!'

'Monstrous! Uncanny! Perfect automata!'

'Capitán, if you had seen them – on that night, and in that dark – I swear you, too, would have read the bill of lading, and thought them real mechanicals, dressed in silk.'

*

There's more to getting a great ship out of harbour than simply freeing the lines to the tugs. It was an hour or more before Captain Percival came to the cabin in which the purser had locked us.

'So,' he said. 'One man without a ticket. One weeping mother found scouring the ship for a daughter called Clarrie. And' – here he raised an eyebrow, for smudged and disordered by wind and rain and Mother's hugs and kisses, Will and I looked like children who'd been at the dress-up bag and painted their faces with burnt sticks – 'and two silk dolls.'

He turned to Mother. 'What is all this about?'

But Mother was as confused as he was. All she could do was show him her ticket and tell him our father was in Australia.

When Uncle Len was asked, he was less help even than that. He lifted his head from his hands only to mutter, 'Me? I was offered a choice of terrors. To go home to face a mother without her only son whom she had left in my care; or risk travelling with him to the dark side of the world.'

'Not dark,' I couldn't help reproving him.

'They're upside down. It's summer there now – full of light and heat.'

'None the less,' snapped Uncle Len, 'you have tricked all of us aboard a ship with only the clothes we stand up in.'

Defensively, my mother drew Will and me closer towards her. 'I've everything I need. And more!'

My brother, too, defended me. 'And Clarrie thought to bring Mother's wedding lines and earrings from the hiding place under the sink.'

Now it was Uncle Len's turn to raise an eyebrow. But then he shrugged. 'You'll have no more need of hiding places, Mary. I made a solemn vow as I was searching the boat for Will: "If I can bring the boy safely back to his mother, I swear I'll never drink or gamble again."'

He looked so forlorn that Will tried to cheer him. 'Don't forget, Uncle, you still have Frozen Billy and Still Lucy.'

'Billy? Lucy? Are there still more of you hidden on my boat?' cried Captain Percival.

'No. They're just dummies.'

Seeing the captain's bewilderment, Uncle Len flicked up the catches of the carrying box and took out Frozen Billy. He slid his hand inside, and then, as if the puppet had just arrived, made introductions.

'Captain Percival, meet Frozen Billy. Now, Frozen Billy, tip your hat politely to Captain Percival.'

'I'm honoured to make your acquaintance,' chirped Frozen Billy as the hand shot up to touch the school cap.

Captain Percival stared at Uncle Len. 'You're a ventriloquist?'

'The very best!' I assured him.

'Top of the Bill at the Alhambra!' crowed my brother.

As usual, the showman in Uncle Len came out on top. He made Frozen Billy pipe up, 'Don't forget me! Len here might be the ventriloquist, but he is nothing – nothing – without the dummy.'

'Or the theatre,' added Uncle Len in his own voice. 'And the audience. But thanks to Clarrie here, we're missing those.'

'Oh, I assure you that you'll get your audience,' said Captain Percival. 'Since you'll be earning your passage, you'll get them every night. What you *won't* get is any pay for your labours.'

He turned to Will. 'What about you?'

'I'm part of the act,' Will said promptly.

'Only till the day you set foot on land,' Mother warned him. 'After that, you'll be back to your schoolbooks, like Clarrie.'

The captain turned to me. 'And you?'

I spread my patchwork skirt wide. 'I can sew.'

'And so can all my sailors. And so can I.'

'And I can cook.'

'And so can the men in my galley.'

'Well, I can—'

But I could think of nothing else that I could do, and the tears flowed.

Mother gathered me into her arms and told the captain proudly, 'Nobody knows how she managed it. But if my Clarrie can get us all safely on a boat to Australia to join her father, then surely she can do *anything*.'

'I have no doubt of it,' said Captain Percival drily. And maybe because he'd been parted too often and too long from his own family to show a marble heart to ours, suddenly his tone softened.

'So, Clarrie, if nobody knows quite how you did it all, then you can begin your punishment by writing your story so even a humble ship's captain can follow it.'

So that's what I do. In notebook after note-book, I'm setting down the story. Mother snatches away each notebook the moment I move on to the next, and I amuse myself by listening to the little cries she lets out as she reads: 'Oh, Clarrie! . . . Oh, my poor love! . . . No, surely not! . . . What courage! . . . You *amaze* me!'

She's not the only person taken up by the thrills of the story. Day by day, Captain Percival strolls by to read the next few pages, and tell me that if my father's any man at all, he will be sterling proud of me.

'Of both of you. I know I would be! Yes. And of your mother too, who did more than most sailors will – stepping off one boat straight onto yet another.' He gives a little smile. 'And Len, who's such a showman I swear he could stop a mutiny simply by picking up one of his puppets!'

He's kind to Mother, too. He's even found her a little job, copying things into the log – so by the time we leave his ship, our family will owe so little for our passage that, with the money Father must have saved, we'll be free to start our lives again before you can blink and say 'Jacaranda!'

Everyone smiles as they watch me hunched over the notebooks, writing and writing. I think Mother sees it as a way of making up for all the time I didn't go to school. But Uncle Len can't help thinking of it as a terrible punishment, so he's forgiven me for tricking him on board.

In any case, he's happy as a bird. He's heard enough from all the other passengers to know he'll make a fine living with the dummies, once we arrive. (I've given him Still Lucy.) When he's not giving shows, he strides up and down the deck, whistling and charming the ladies. Today he wheedled me into darning a few of the holes in his clothes. 'Hurry up, Clarrie! Even the poor devils in steerage need amusing. I've promised them a few moments with Still Lucy before my show for the nobs tonight, and I must look my best.'

'Plenty of time,' I assure him, and he grins.

'Clarrie, even this endless voyage will be over before I trust your word again.'

I hang my head and blush, in part from

shame, in part from pride. After all, if I'd not been 'Good Clarrie! Good girl, Clarrie!' all those years, somebody might well have noticed when I began to take my family's fortune in my hand, and risk it all to get our heart's desire.

And so I sit on deck, raising my head every few minutes to watch the cormorants that follow us. The girl on the cocoa tin smiles at me as I lift the lid to take out my pen, or the needles and threads that one of the sailors has lent me. This tin is my only possession in the world now, and yet my smile's as wide as hers.

Mother leans over the rail to stare down at where the *Fresh Hope*'s steep bows slice through the water. When I come near, she reaches out an arm to draw me closer.

Together we watch the wide waves part.

'Just twelve days more!' she tells me. 'Captain Percival said he thinks it will be only twelve days more.'

I tell you honestly. I cannot *wait*.

I'll put the notebooks back now, on the jacaranda shelf Will carved for the youngest of our baby sisters, along with the pretty painted cocoa tin, and the strange stones that Father and I found one day while we were walking along the creek.

ABOUT THE AUTHOR

ANNE FINE was born in Leicester.
She went to Wallisdean County Primary School in Fareham,
Hampshire, and then to Northampton High School for Girls.
She read Politics and History at the University of Warwick
and then worked as an information officer for Oxfam before
teaching (very briefly!) in a Scottish prison.
She started her first book during a blizzard that stopped her
getting to Edinburgh City Library and has been
writing ever since.

ANNE FINE is now a hugely popular and celebrated author.
Among the many awards she has won are
the *Carnegie Medal* (twice), the *Whitbread Children's
Novel Award* (twice), the *Guardian Children's Literature Award*
and a *Smarties Prize*. She has twice been voted
Children's Writer of the Year at the *British Book Awards*
and was the Children's Laureate for 2001-2003.

She has written over forty books for young people,
including *Goggle-Eyes, Flour Babies, Bill's New Frock,
The Tulip Touch* and *Madame Doubtfire*.
She has also written a number of titles for adult readers,
and has edited three poetry collections.

Anne Fine lives in County Durham and has two
daughters and a large hairy dog called Harvey.

www.annefine.co.uk

anne Fine

Bad Dreams

Stories in books aren't real, are they?

Mel loves reading. She prefers books to people.
New girl Imogen is *frightened* of books.
And only Mel can stop Imogen's private
horror story – stop the bad dreams . . .

'A super four-star read' SUNDAY TIMES

'Beautifully plotted' TELEGRAPH

'Quirky but gripping' TES

SHORTLISTED FOR THE W H SMITH CHILDREN'S BOOK OF THE YEAR

0 440 86732 0
978 0440 86732 6

aNNE FiNE

Charm School

Who cares if flower earrings are 'Totally Yesterday'?

Bonny doesn't.
Nor does she want to know how to bleach
her elbows.
She only wants to make new friends.
But the other girls at Charm School are so
self-obsessed.
And they'll do *anything* to win the much-coveted
'Glistering Tiara'...

'A chuckle a line' INDEPENDENT

'Assured and lively . . . a clarion call against the idea
that girls should simply be decorative' SUNDAY TIMES

'All of Fine's usual pace and verve' TES

0 440 86731 2
978 0440 86731 9

ANNE FINE

The More the Merrier

Three days of family fun?

Cousin Titania is writing soppy notes to Santa.
Uncle Tristram is chucking potatoes at the cat.
And Mum is on the verge of a breakdown.
Ralph is *not* having a good Christmas . . .

'A wickedly seasonal tale' THE TIMES

'Anne Fine at her wittiest' TES

'There's a grim cast in this hilarious but barbed
story of how Christmas can go so wrong for
so many people' GUARDIAN

0 440 86733 9
978 0440 86733 3